A Great Day for Ice Cream

K.E. Bosley

K.E.B. Press

Dedication

To my son, Evan (Ironis)
You never stop surprising me

.

Acknowledgments

This book wouldn't have been possible without the help of publishing professionals, family, friends, and of course, those strange, unexpected, real-life plot twists that we all encounter in life. Those experiences are the inspiration behind my writing.

First, I owe much gratitude to everyone who gave motivating, uplifting, or helpful comments on one or more of my stories, including Alan A. Allen, Patricia Andrews-Keenan, Sue Campbell, Jami Carpenter, Montego Craddock, Guy Dawson, Brandon Gallegos, Tonya Hampton, Giovanna Salas, Becky Schrader, Margaret Schrader, and Jillian White. Your time and your remarks—whether short or detailed—meant everything. I'm sorry if I missed anyone!

Thank you, Richard Moore, for always reminding me to finish my book.

I want to acknowledge Suzanne Campbell, the book designer behind my book. After I viewed the cover proof, I was a bit emotional; it looked so darn good. Suzanne's creative vision for book designing is an absolute gift.

I'm extremely grateful to Jami Carpenter. Meeting Jami at the writers' conference in 2021 was meant to be. Her insight and vast knowledge on publishing, editing, and love for grammar provided me with an enormous amount of editorial and publishing support. I can't thank you enough for helping me throughout this simple, yet, tough publishing process.

Finally, to my family, the super glue that keeps it together. I would like to thank my parents for their unconditional love and prayers. I want to thank my siblings and nieces for their support and for helping me to promote my book. To my grandfather, who worked for over 50 years at the *Madison Journal*, typing stories, uploading photos, and running the press, you have genuinely inspired me. I am truly your granddaughter.

Contents

A Great Day for Ice Cream

Finally … it's back in stock! And it's on sale! Yep, it's going to be a great day for ice cream, Tiff thought. She eagerly arrived at her favorite grocery store knowing she'd soon be taking home her favorite ice cream: Chunky Monkey.

"I better stock up in case they run out again," Tiff said to no one in particular. She reached for a shopping basket just as another customer reached for the same basket.

"Ladies first," the man said with an unusual accent.

Tiff found his voice hypnotic and the smell of his woody scented cologne manly, yet quite romantic.

"Thank you," said Tiff.

Tiff reminded herself, *I'm only here for ice cream. Keep your eyes on the ice cream.*

Tiff greeted a few grocery workers before

heading toward the frozen section. From a short distance away, she saw the same man with the soothing voice placing a few pints of ice cream in his cart.

She arrived at the frozen ice cream section. "This is not looking good. I do not see my ice cream," Tiff said.

She opened the freezer door to get a better look as the fog on the windows made it difficult to clearly see inside. She still did not see it. She began moving frozen items around hoping to find a carton sitting behind other flavors, yet she still did not see it.

"This is really not good. I was told they restocked this morning. Where is my ice cream? It can't be gone that fast! I can't believe they're out … again," she pouted.

She let out another long sigh, then caught a whiff of the cologne on the man she bumped into earlier.

"Give the Chubby Hubby a try," his voice soothed.

Tiff turned around and saw his liquid eyes smiling at hers. She thought, *If he's trying to flirt with that Chubby Hubby line, it's not working.*

Puzzled, Tiff asked, "Excuse me?"

The man picked up a pint of ice cream and directed it to Tiff. "The Chubby Hubby … as in

Chubby Hubby ice cream, of course."

"Oh. No thanks. I'm devoted to my Chunky Monkey." Tiff smiled and walked away.

Still disappointed that her ice cream was sold out, Tiff decided to browse the store to see if she needed anything else or perhaps would come across a misplaced Chunky Monkey ice cream container. Just as she pushed her cart to the next aisle, she accidentally bumped it into the same man's cart.

"Oh, pardon me, Miss," he said.

"No worries … my cart actually hit yours," Tiff admitted.

He looked at her basket and started to chuckle.

"I'm sorry, but what could possibly be so funny?" Tiff asked.

"Well, I get that you're truly devoted to your Chunky Monkey ice cream, but there are other food items in the store you actually might enjoy."

"I beg your pardon? What does that mean?" she asked.

"Well, I couldn't help but notice that your cart is still empty."

"Well, maybe because I don't want anything except for my ice cream, but they're sold out. Besides, I'm browsing in case I do find something."

"Sorry they didn't have what you want, but perhaps you'll come across something you need," said the man.

"Well, I've been a regular customer here for years—a faithful one, not to mention—and they're sold out of my favorite ice cream, and that's just unusual," Tiff said.

"It's still pretty early in the day, and anything is possible. Things may seem bad, but something good usually comes out of it."

"I guess you have a point. Well, I better get back to browsing," Tiff responded.

Tiff strolled away actually feeling warm and cheerful. She decided to go back and try that Chubby Hubby ice cream after all. She had no doubt this man's positive outlook had a lot to do with it. His words did not sound like philosophical babble.

She arrived back at the frozen section, opened the freezer door, and grabbed a pint of Chubby Hubby ice cream. She told herself, *It doesn't look too bad*. She turned the carton over and read the ingredients. "Hmmm, a bit different from my Chunky Monkey, but I'll give it a try."

Just as she was about to place the ice cream in her basket, she caught the same man staring at her. He moved closer and looked in her cart.

"Don't worry. Chunky Monkey will understand."

They looked at each other and couldn't help but laugh.

"You know, if we keep running into each other like this, we'll have to go out on a date … maybe for some ice cream?" the man asked.

"Well, if it's Chunky Monkey, maybe I'll take you up on that offer," said Tiff.

She walked away feeling happier and more energized than ever as she strolled through one more aisle before heading out. As she approached the checkout, she let out a chuckle at the day's disappointing yet somehow satisfying shopping experience. "Never in a million years would I have thought I would be going home with Chubby Hubby Ice Cream," said Tiff.

As she stood in line waiting to pay for a few items, she visually scanned the other checkouts hoping to see the man one last time, but she did not see him.

She approached the cashier, reached for her ice cream, and placed it on the counter. As she dug into her purse, her wallet slipped out of her hand and fell to the floor. She bent down to pick up her wallet and suddenly heard a soothing voice behind her addressing the cashier.

"Excuse me, Sir. I was just at this checkout and thought all the ice cream I purchased was

Chubby Hubby. I didn't realize one was Chunky Monkey."

Tiff looked up and smiled.

"Well, now. It looks like it's a great day for ice cream," said the man.

But, You Told Me

"*H*ey Wendy, will you check this amount?" asked the restaurant hostess.

"Sure." Wendy used a mini computer-like machine to verify a high roller's complimentary ticket. "Here you go. It's valued at $100."

"Thanks."

Friday nights were busy for the Bistro Flair. The high-end restaurant was filled with local high rollers and wealthy tourists looking for a fine dining experience.

As Wendy waited to check another ticket, she noticed a tall, well-dressed man grinning at her. He was standing with a much older and quite sophisticated looking couple waiting to be seated.

Wendy returned a faint smile, turned away, and casually glanced back at the party of three, particularly the classy looking man.

They definitely don't look like locals I've ever

seen; more like royalty, if you ask me. Maybe they're here for a wedding or some big event.

As a hostess escorted the elegant group to a table, the classy man kept grinning at Wendy.

He's even more handsome close up.

Minutes after the group was settled at their table, the stylish man stood up and walked toward Wendy. "Excuse me, miss. Can you direct me to the restroom?"

As her head gazed up, Wendy's eyes widened. "Hi … yes, it's just out the entrance, on your left."

The man beamed, "Thanks."

Oh my goodness, he smells good … and there's nothing like a grown, well-dressed man with a sexy beard. I wonder how old he is.

When the man returned, he approached Wendy for a second time.

"Hi again." He stared at her name badge. "So, what do you do here, Wendy?"

"I'm a complimentary assistant."

The man gave her a curious stare.

"I basically make sure gamblers and high rollers have a good dining experience. If you don't mind me asking, who's the couple at your table; your parents?" asked Wendy.

"Yep, they're celebrating their anniversary

and catching a late show later tonight."

"Ah that's sweet. How many years?"

"Thirty, as a matter of fact," said the man.

"Well, they look really good," exclaimed Wendy.

The man smiled. "I'll make sure to tell them. Well, I better get back. It was nice talking with you, Wendy."

Wendy couldn't deny the captivating energy she felt from his presence. His style intrigued her. The smell of his expensive cologne, his perfectly tailored clothing, and his charming disposition aroused her interest. She wanted to know more about this mysterious stranger and his parents.

~

The family of three finished their meal and waited for the check. The fashionable man strolled toward Wendy for a third time.

"It was nice meeting you. How about we meet again tomorrow for lunch?"

Wendy attempted to play hard to get. "I don't even know your name."

The man put out his hand. "My name is Ben."

Wendy shook his hand. "Nice to meet you, Ben, but I still don't know anything about you."

"Then how about we exchange numbers, and you'll know everything about me."

"Hmm, well, I really have just one question: how old are you?" Wendy asked.

"Just turned twenty-five; is that too young for you?"

Although Wendy was only a year older, dating someone younger, even if it was by a single year, was definitely a deal-breaker. But she wanted to know more about the mystery man and gave in.

She wrote her number down on a sticky note and handed it to him. "I'm off weekends."

Over the next several weeks, Wendy and Ben ate lunch at the finest restaurants. She was impressed by his amazing taste in food and his accomplishments as an architect. He was the most cultured, well-dressed, and well-mannered man she had ever dated. Yet, that 'too good to be true' vibe started to creep in her thoughts.

"That was so delicious! You always find the best places to eat," exclaimed Wendy.

"Glad you liked it. So, after we leave here I was thinking we could visit my parents. They have friends and family in town, and I'd like to introduce you to them. You'll be the first woman I've ever invited over. I hope you don't mind," said Ben.

"Sure, I'd love to meet your parents!"

Nonetheless, she was surprised by the invitation.

A woman meeting a man's parents was a big deal in Wendy's opinion—it was a sure sign that he really liked her. She felt excited about the idea and didn't hesitate, realizing this would be a great opportunity to know more about him.

Thirty minutes later, they drove up to a luxury home. Wendy's assessment was spot on; everything about this family was exclusive.

Ben was a complete gentleman, jumping out of a Range Rover and opening the passenger door, just as Wendy expected.

After stepping out of the vehicle, she stood motionless. "Wow, this house is absolutely gorgeous. I'm excited to meet everyone!"

Ben locked hands with Wendy. "Oh, you know what? I just remembered they went to a show and won't be back until later. Come on, let's go in. I have a key."

Wendy's mouth dropped as she entered the expensive home. It had an old Hollywood appeal combined with the lavish style of an elegant penthouse.

Wendy turned and looked at Ben. "This house is like, wow, so gorgeous. Now I feel nervous about meeting them. Do I need to curtsy?"

Ben laughed and continued to hold her hand. "Relax. It's okay. Come check this out." He guided her to an elegant stone fireplace with two angled piers reaching close to fifteen feet high.

"This is breathtaking. I've never seen a fireplace like this before," Wendy said.

"And you never will … I designed it for my parents. Let's have a seat."

Wendy sat close to Ben on an expensive Fendi Casa couch. As they held hands, Ben leaned in for a kiss, which almost turned into a make-out session.

Wendy pulled away. "Wait, this is weird. We're in your parents' home."

Ben attempted to kiss her again but was pushed away. "What wrong? It's not like we're naked. Besides, no one else is here."

Wendy pulled back. "I know, but …"

They were interrupted by the sound of a male and female voice. Ben's face transformed from romantic to shocking.

The sound of the voices grew closer.

Ben stood up. "Mother, Father, I thought you we're going out of town today?"

Wendy thought, *Out of town? But, he told me his parents went to a show.*

Ben's father looked disappointed. "We had to cancel because of an unexpected storm. By the way, did you use my Range Rover again?"

His Dad's Range Rover? But, he told me that was his car.

Ben's mother reached for a hug. "Honey, next time get your father's permission." Ben's mother stared at Wendy. "And who is this young lady? She looks awfully familiar."

Ben's voice was jumpy. "Mother, Father … this is Wendy. Wendy, these are my parents."

"Oh yes, you're that lovely waitress from the restaurant. It's nice to see you again, dear," said his mother.

Wendy tried to conceal her surprise. "Actually, I'm a complimentary assistant. It's a pleasure meeting you both."

There was an awkward pause as Ben's parents appeared to be confused.

Wendy attempted to break the uncomfortable silence. "Your home is … it's so beautiful."

"Thank you again, dear," said Ben's mother.

Wendy continued, "And I've never seen a fireplace like this before."

"Oh, yes. Isn't it lovely?" Ben's mother turned and admired the beautiful fireplace. "Ben's father is an Architectural Project Manager and designed this many years ago. It was a gift for our wedding anniversary," she explained.

Wendy was perplexed. *Ben's father designed it? But Ben told me he designed it.*

Sweat poured from Ben's forehead like raindrops. He grabbed Wendy's hand. "Sorry, Mother. Sorry, Father. We were just about to leave."

"Honey, are you alright? You're perspiring like crazy!" his mother said.

Ben wiped his forehead. "I'm fine, Mom. This sweater is making me hot."

"Well, we're heading out, too, just as soon as we unpack and freshen up," said Ben's father. "Your mother and I decided to eat at the Bistro Flair again this evening."

"That place is exquisite. When we were there last Thursday, we celebrated Ben's 18th birthday, but tonight, my husband and I will be celebrating our twenty-year wedding anniversary. It was nice meeting you dear ... and Ben, will you please make sure you do something about those pets in your room. They keep getting out of their cages," his mother chided.

Wendy turned and glared at Ben, fuming. "But, you told me ..."

Close Case

"Good morning. I'm Jessie Baker. I have a ten o'clock appointment with Detective Garson."

"Hi. Sure. Go ahead and have a seat. He'll be right with you," said a receptionist.

Jessie was eager to meet the detective. After their initial phone call, she felt confident that he would be able to help her find her biological mother.

"Ms. Baker? Hi. I'm Detective Garson."

Jessie couldn't have been more wrong guessing his physical appearance. From the sound of his voice on the phone, she pictured a tall, lean man. Instead, he was average height and slightly stocky.

Jessie stood up. "Detective Garson … hi; it's so nice to meet you."

The detective shook Jessie's hand. "My office is just down the hall to the right."

15

Jessie grabbed her folder and followed.

As they walked into the office, the detective directed Jessie to a chair. "Please have a seat. I must admit this is one of the most interesting cases I've come across in a long time. Were you able to get your adoption records or any other information?"

Jessie handed the detective a folder. "Well, my adoptive parents left me the house and I have the information my adoptive mom shared before her death: that I was left on a doorstep with a note from my biological mother. The note said something about her boyfriend had died and that she was only able to care for one child."

The detective took forms out of the folder and examined them for a brief moment. "Because we're limited on facts, I'll need to conduct extensive research and interviews. The process could take days, weeks, even months."

"I understand," replied Jessie.

"I'll get started right away but let me know if you come across any additional information. It doesn't matter if it's small or strange. Anything could be a tip," replied the detective.

Driving home, Jessie tried to think of something, any kind of clue that might help the detective with the investigation. She decided to recheck every stored box in her late adoptive parents' home.

This is going to take forever. I'll have to go through a few every night.

Later that evening, Jessie opened a large box, and was overwhelmed with nostalgia. Seeing an old dress that belonged to her adoptive mother made Jessie feel like a teenager all over again. It was the dress she had worn to celebrate Jessie's sixteenth birthday.

Jessie never realized how fast time flew while reminiscing over precious childhood memories. She took a deep breath and exhaled. "Whew! I'll look through one more of these cartons and call it a night."

While searching through a small box, Jessie noticed a picture sticking out from some of the items. She looked closer and gasped.

"Oh my ... this is ... me. I mean, it has to be, when I was a baby. My parents must have taken a picture of me after I was left on their doorstep. And that must be the note from my biological mother taped to the side of the baby carrier."

She stopped for a minute, wondering if her youthful years would have been the same or different had her birth mom never given her up.

Jessie went back to work, digging through

the box hoping to find more information, but with no luck.

Jessie placed everything back in the box except for the picture. "I'll give the detective a call first thing tomorrow morning."

~

The following afternoon, the investigator arrived at Jessie's home.

"Hi, Detective Garson, come in. So I found this picture in one of the storage boxes. Unfortunately, I didn't find anything else."

The detective sat down on the sofa and pulled out a magnifier to closely inspect the picture. What he came across next astonished him.

He handed Jessie the magnifier. "Take a look at this. Do you see the initials engraved on the front of the shoes?"

"Yes, I see … um … it looks like the initials J.G. The 'J' must stand for Jessie. So the note left on the baby seat must have had my first name. But what does the letter 'G' stand for?" asked Jessie.

The detective took a long breath. "My mom raised me as a single parent. When I was about sixteen, my mother met a man, a good man. They eventually married just as I was about to turn eighteen, so it didn't make any sense to

K

take his last name."

Jessie raised her eyebrows far enough to touch her hairline as she listened to the detective.

The detective continued. "Before I jetted off to college, I helped them move into a new home. My mom kept so much stuff. Anyway, I came across a pair of baby shoes with the initials J.G. in that exact same color. They were tucked away in a small box."

Jessie's fingers started to tremble and her heart raced. "Detective, what are you saying?"

The detective turned to Jessie. "My first name is Jackson, and I think you're my twin sister."

Dear Jury

"**W**ould you hold that door, please?" Staci hurried toward the elevator.

A man wearing a dark-colored grey suit held the door. "Of course, what floor?"

"Nine, please. Thank you," replied Staci.

After several seconds of silence, a weird sensation came over her, causing an undeniable urge to speak with the distinguished-looking fellow.

"You know, I find it rather eerie that we're the only two people in this elevator," said Staci.

"I'm harmless," said the man.

Staci giggled. "No ... I meant that it's strange because we're in a courthouse elevator ... on a Monday morning. I would have expected a crowd of people."

Just as Staci finished her statement, the elevator stopped on the 3rd floor. An older man in a navy suit carrying a briefcase, stepped in.

"Mr. Morris … ready for another great week?" asked the much older man.

Staci thought, *So his name is Mr. Morris.*

"Always … strong team you've got there," replied Mr. Morris.

"Yep, and they're getting younger. See you later." The elevator stopped on the 5th floor and the older man stepped out.

As the elevator door shut and proceeded to move up, Staci tried to think of another way to start a conversation.

Maybe I can ask if he's an attorney. What a silly question. Of course he's an attorney … look at him; he's in a freshly pressed suit, carrying a briefcase … in a court building.

As Staci tried to think of another query, she actually found herself enjoying the comfortable silence and dropped the idea of asking anything.

Seconds later, Staci reached inside her purse to find some mints. As she dug through her bag, a few items fell on the floor.

"Oh great … why did I decide to bring this small purse?" mumbled Staci.

Before she could reach down to retrieve her things, the man was already kneeling to assist.

As Staci extended her hand for her belongings, their eyes locked just enough for her to notice the warmth of his eyes.

"Thank you," replied Staci.

"Of course," responded the gentleman.

Staci joked. "Your briefcase is a lot bigger than my purse. You want to trade?"

The man gave a faint smile. "Sorry, not today."

The elevator stopped and opened on the ninth floor.

"After you," said the gentleman.

"Thank you," replied Staci.

Staci stepped out of the elevator and walked briskly toward the restroom to touch up her hair and make-up.

Minutes later, Staci approached the area outside of the courtroom. She waited among the other potential jurors to enter.

"I hope this will be quick," said a potential female juror.

"If I'm selected, this will be my first time serving. I'm kind of excited," replied Staci.

Before the two women could engage in a longer conversation, a bailiff walked out of the courtroom, made an announcement, and presented the court rules.

As the prospective jurors were escorted inside the courtroom, Staci saw Mr. Morris, the same man from the elevator.

Staci and a few others were led up a few steps and seated in a jury box.

The judge explained the nature of the case, then proceeded to question each potential juror. After calling out several names, the judge finally made his way to Staci.

"Ms. Hill, it has come to my attention that there was contact between you and Mr. Morris. Is that correct?"

Hearing her name spoken by the judge, Staci's heart started beating fast.

"Uh, that's correct, your Honor," replied Staci.

"It is very important that any incident occurring between an attorney and a juror have no effect on his or her ability to be fair and impartial. Do you understand, Ms. Hill?"

"Yes, Sir," replied Staci.

"How did you and Mr. Morris meet?"

"We met in the elevator … this morning. I asked him to hold the door," replied Staci.

"Do you believe this incident will have any effect on your ability to be fair and impartial?" asked the judge.

"No, Sir. I … I don't believe so," said Staci.

"What was your impression of Mr. Morris?"

"Well, I thought he was polite … and well-dressed," replied Staci.

"What was your conversation like with Mr. Morris?" the judge asked.

Please let this be the last question.

"It was not much of a conversation. Just small talk ... like how empty it was in the elevator. Oh, and I asked if he wanted to trade his briefcase for my purse," replied Staci.

The other potential jurors chuckled.

"And why on earth would you ask such a question?" asked the judge.

"Well, it was just a joke because while I was trying to find some mints a few items fell out of my small purse. Mr. Morris was a gentleman and helped me pick them up."

"I see. Just one more question, Ms. Hill," the judge announced.

Oh, thank goodness.

"Do you find Mr. Morris attractive?"

Staci felt perspiration leaking from her armpits. The skin on her face felt hot as if a blow torch was inches away.

"Excuse me, your Honor?" asked Staci.

"Would you go on a date with Mr. Morris?"

A few of the potential jurors snickered and giggled. Staci's face now felt like it was on fire. Her heart beat even faster. She felt trapped and embarrassed. The uncomfortable position she found herself in along with wanting to be on a jury kept her from telling the judge the truth.

"Ms. Hill. You appear to be flustered," remarked the judge.

"I apologize, Your Honor … I … well, he's not my type," replied Staci.

Mr. Morris abruptly approached the judge. After several minutes of whispers between the judge and Mr. Morris, the conversation stopped. Mr. Morris walked back to the bench, and there was a stern—yet amused—look on the judge's face as he stared at Staci.

"Ms. Hill, you're excused from this jury. The court attendant will escort you out with further instructions."

Staci was mortified. A variety of emotions overwhelmed her: anger, embarrassment, even relief, though the idea of not being able to serve on a jury was a disappointment.

The Following Day

Staci was still feeling the disappointing effects as a result of her actions in the courtroom. She decided an explanation and apology were necessary, and what better way to accomplish that than by writing a letter.

Staci sat down on her computer and started typing. In her letter, she mentioned that Mr. Morris was indeed someone she would date and that she found him to be attractive, but she desperately wanted the opportunity to serve as a first time juror.

A Week Later

Staci received a call from her cousin, Tiff. "Hey Staci, had to see how you were holding up since the whole court incident."

"I'm okay, just can't believe it happened."

"Well, if this makes you feel any better, someone reminded that sometimes good things can come out of what appears to be bad."

"And would this someone happen to be the Chubby Hubby guy you met in the grocery store?" asked Staci.

"It's amazing what missing ice cream can lead to," explained Tiff.

The two women chuckled.

The anxiety Staci felt over the last several days intensified but her cousin always found a way to lift her mood. Their conversation was interrupted by an incoming call. "Hey Tiff, I need to take this."

As Staci ended the call with her cousin and clicked over, she wasn't sure what to expect, but receiving a phone call personally from the judge was not one of them.

"Judge Jenkins. Thank you for reading my letter and taking time out of your busy schedule to call. I just wanted to say that I know what I did was wrong, and I am truly sorry for causing any disruptions to the jury selection."

"Ms. Hill, some potential jurors will try anything to get out of serving, but you wanted to serve. So, I thank you for that, although the truth is always the best. However, you still would have been dismissed from serving as a juror on that case," said the judge.

"What? But why?" asked Staci.

"Ms. Hill, I've been a judge for over three decades and have seen many things in a courtroom, but nothing like I witnessed that day. You see, Mr. Morris asked for your removal, and quite frankly, it was a smart decision. Having you on that bench would have been a major distraction for him and we absolutely cannot have that kind of interference in a courtroom.

Staci was at a loss for words.

"Now I have to get back to work, but one more thing, Ms. Hill?"

"Yes, Sir," replied Staci.

"Mr. Morris is single and that case is closed."

Hell Hath No Fury
Like a Woman Divorced

*E*very day after work, Mike, a tire salesman, purchased lottery scratch tickets, hoping to win a few million.

One day, his dreams became a reality. A lucky scratch ticket landed him five million dollars—before taxes. From then on, only two things were on his mind. The first was being with the young beautiful model named Bella he met online … who happened to live in France. The second was to never ever tell his wife, Ruth, about his lucky scratch ticket. Keeping the money and splurging it on the attractive French woman was his ultimate goal.

So, he came up with a plan: before receiving the money he would divorce his spouse and then pursue the gorgeous French woman. After several days perfecting his scheme, he decided it was time to announce his decision.

"Look, I want a divorce," said Mike. He threw papers down on the kitchen counter. "Here."

"What? What is this?" asked Ruth.

"I just told you. I want a divorce."

"Uh huh ... well, I guess I should be surprised but I'm not. Tell me, is it because I'm not as skinny as the girls on that dating site you keep checking out?" Ruth asked.

Mike looked shocked. "How did you ... you've been spying on my phone?"

"Of course not. I may be a heavy woman, but it doesn't mean I'm slow," said Ruth.

"Look, I'm just not attracted to you any more, okay?" replied Mike.

"Well, that's pretty obvious. You haven't touched me in months. Oh, and the list just keeps going. Tell me something, Mike. Were you ever attracted to me? Did you ever love me or were you just using me?" asked Ruth.

"Look, no kids ... married for three years, plus, not much in the bank. It's your house; you keep it. It'll make for an easy and quick divorce," said Mike.

"Well, you clearly made your choice."

"I'll be packing some of my things and staying with a coworker," said Mike.

"Sounds like you got this all perfectly

planned out," said Ruth. She picked up the papers, walked to the bedroom, and slammed the door.

Mike showed no concern whatsoever. He opened the fridge, grabbed a soda, and sat on the couch. He released a big sigh of relief knowing he would soon be a divorced millionaire with that young, slim online goodie by his side.

Four weeks later, their divorce was official. Mike couldn't wait to share the details of all the things he was going to do. He logged on to his dating account and sent a message:

"Hey beautiful ... got a lot to celebrate. I want to see you soon. I'll be able to buy you whatever you want." He continued to brag about all the things he planned on giving her. He even promised the young beauty that he would pay for her modeling career.

A week later, the money finally made it to Mike's account. The first thing he did was rent an expensive condo followed by the purchase of a luxury vehicle and designer clothes. He sent thousands of dollars to his dream girl, as promised.

While he engaged in lavish spending, the thought of his ex-wife never came to his mind. During their marriage, he somehow convinced his wife to spend her money on things that he felt were important, such as the latest high tech gadgets, all for his personal needs, yet he never made any attempt to pay her back one penny of the money she spent on him.

For days, Mike tried to meet the French beauty, purchasing a plane ticket to France, but there was no success, as he did not hear from her. He was desperate to meet her, and despite giving her most of his winnings, his replies went unanswered. Yet he still heavily pursued the woman. He promised to buy her diamonds if he could meet. He even purchased a ticket for his beautiful Bella to meet him in his country, yet still no response.

For many more heartbreaking days, his messages remained unread. He was hurt and angry, but things got much worse .... the worst of all days when the account of his lover-to-be suddenly closed. She was nowhere to be found.

The next day Ruth received a call from her sister. "You're not going to believe this. I just found out that before you two were even divorced your ex won five million dollars. I can't believe he hid all that money from you."

"It's fine; there's no money ... and no Bella."

Love at Second Flight

"Now boarding C1-30."

Janine was the first in line and handed her ticket to the female attendant at the counter. "Thanks," she said and walked down the jetway toward the plane.

As the passengers filed in, Janine headed for her seat and found she was in center seat between two men. One appeared to be in his early 60s, while the other seemed a bit closer to her age.

"Do you mind if I squeeze in?" she asked.

"Not at all," they said, and the elderly gentleman moved his feet to oblige.

"Thank you," said Janine. She settled into her seat and checked her phone one more time before putting it in airplane mode.

The gentleman next to the window turned to her. "So you're a sci-fi fan?" the man asked.

"I'm sorry?" asked Janine.

The man pointed to the book on her lap.

"Oh, yes, I guess I am. Or should I say, science fiction addict."

"Well, you won't be disappointed. That book's got a lot of action," said the man.

"So you're also a sci-fi fan?" asked Janine.

"Absolutely and a fan of numbers; I'm Curtis."

"Nice meeting you. I'm Janine."

"A pleasure," said Curtis.

After chatting for over an hour, Curtis asked, "So, I don't mean to pry but are you headed to Dallas or Maryland?"

"Well, I've never been to Maryland. I'm going to Dallas ... for a job interview. I've got one offer on the table right here in California but thought it wouldn't hurt to check out my options," said Janine.

"Wow, good luck! 1,200 miles of daily commute won't be so bad, unless you're driving; then we're talking 23 hours." Curtis and Janine both chuckled.

"So, what's the position?" Curtis asked.

"Data scientist," said Janine.

"Ah ha ... that explains the book."

"You got it. So, are you going to Maryland or Dallas?" asked Janine.

"Maryland. I was hoping to avoid any stops, but at least I don't have to change planes. Anyway, I'm helping my aunt move. She's a widow living in a huge house and wants to downsize," said Curtis.

"Well, aren't you the helpful nephew."

~

"Boy, time sure does fly—no pun intended; it looks like you'll be in Dallas in 2,700 seconds," said Curtis.

"I see what you mean by being a fan of numbers," said Janine.

"Well, I teach math, so numbers just keep coming out. What I love most about numbers is that any problem can be solved, even life problems. Take your interviews, for instance. You are sitting on two possible offers. Then you'll have to weigh your options by looking at all the positives and negatives," said Curtis

"Hmm … interesting, you've managed to combine 'weigh, positives, and negatives,' all very important mathematical terms, into one sentence," said Janine.

Janine and Curtis chuckled and continued talking the remainder of the flight to Dallas.

~

"Well, this is my stop. It was really nice chatting with you, Curtis, and good luck with helping your aunt move," said Janine.

"Likewise, and good luck with the interview."

As Janine grabbed her bag and walked off the plane, she felt a delightful burst of energy followed by a strange sense of sadness. She wished that she could somehow continue the conversation with Curtis but she was also anxious to get to her job interview.

Four days later, Janine was back at the airport waiting to catch her flight home. She recalled everything about her visit to Dallas. She was pleased with the second interview and excited about the wonderful opportunities both jobs presented, yet she was undecided as to which position she should accept. The exuberant feeling from seconds ago quickly changed to an emotionless sensation.

Janine whispered to herself, *Oh Lord, please give me a sign.* She suddenly had a flashback of Curtis and their delightful conversation.

"Now boarding A1-30," said the gate attendant.

After showing her boarding pass, Janine stepped in the plane and saw Curtis in an aisle seat near the back, reading. She headed toward him.

"Excuse me, by any chance are you reading *Snow Watch*?" asked Janine.

"Wow! This is incredible! I'm a mathematician

but never would have guessed the odds of seeing you again, let alone on this flight. I thought you were flying back a couple of days ago!" exclaimed Curtis.

Janine sat next to him in a center seat. "Yeah, I decided to stay a few days and do the tour thing and check out homes in case I ended up relocating. So how did the moving go?"

"It was smooth. I think I must have taken after my aunt in the math and science department. She made the transition very easy for everyone. Everything was packed and arranged by weight, size, you name it. She's a smart old lady, that's for sure. So the important question is ... how did the interview go?" asked Curtis.

"Well, they offered me the job."

"Congrats! Who's the lucky employer?"

~

About a year later, as Janine sat at the airport waiting to board the plane, Curtis came up behind her with a bottle of water.

"Thank you," she giggled.

"Tell me. I need a good laugh after waiting in that line," said Curtis.

"I was just thinking ... the last time we were on a plane together, I had two job offers. What were the odds that you and I would both be working at the same college?" asked Janine.

"You mean, more specifically, the odds of two people meeting twice on a plane? For the first time, I'm not even sure I can answer that … just happy that the odds were in our favor," Curtis said, caressing Janine's hands.

"Now boarding C31-60," said the gate agent.

"Hmm, let's wait. Don't worry; we have assigned seats," said Curtis.

Janine and Curtis were the last two passengers to board. They handed over their tickets and headed toward the plane's entrance. As they got closer to their assigned seats, Curtis called out Janine's name.

"I know we've only been dating for nine months or 212.917 days, but exactly 365 days ago, we met on an airplane and somehow crossed paths four days later on another airplane," Curtis said, getting down on one knee.

The other passengers were pleasantly surprised. Janine couldn't hear anyone or anything except for Curtis. She was in a trance.

"I don't want another millisecond to go by without you in my life. Will you have me?" he asked.

"For infinity," cried Janine.

Curtis stood up and they hugged each other tightly. Passengers cheered and a handful were in tears. A couple sitting directly across from them congratulated them and chatted with Curtis while a passenger sitting in front of Janine caught her attention.

"How sweet … you two met on a plane. Is that when you discovered you were in love?"

"Yes, we met on a plane, but it was love at second flight."

Manuscript in the Guest Room

"My manuscript! I've looked everywhere. Where is it? Where is it, Laura? What have you done with my manuscript?!"
Winston frowned, clenching both fists against his forehead.

"Winston? What's happening? What are you talking about?"Laura asked, following her husband up the wood-trimmed stairs.

"I know you've done something to it. Now tell me where it is ... right now!" Winston's voice grew angrier and heavier as he threw a blanket on the hardwood floor in their master bedroom.

"I dare not touch your manuscript. I haven't seen it. I don't know where it is. Please believe me!" Laura's eyes widened in disbelief as she stared at her husband. He seemed to have gone mad.

Writing was Winston's passion and Laura

knew how much he adored it. She never disturbed her husband while he was writing nor did she ever touch his manuscripts unless instructed to.

"Three long years, thousands of hours of writing, and now gone. Do you have any idea what you've done? Do you? You've ruined me. You've destroyed me," Winston yelled.

Guilt suddenly appeared to overpower Laura's distress. Knowing that her husband's manuscript may be gone ... forever ... was becoming too much to bear. She started to wonder if perhaps she had done something to the manuscript without realizing it.

"But I swear I've never seen it. Oh, Winston dear, I feel so terrible that it's missing. I'm sure we will find it. It has to be here."

"Oh, you swear? Well, how about promising to be a better wife! You know? I think you're jealous. I think you intentionally hid my manuscript. You're always complaining about why I don't pay attention to you, why we don't have dinner together anymore, why I need to start a new manuscript whenever I've completed another. Why, why, why. Well, if you think you have won by getting my attention, then I'm afraid it did not work." Winston rolled his eyes.

"Winston, you know I would never do such a thing. I've been a devoted wife for eight years and would never ever betray you. I've been a good wife. I have. I simply ask but never complain. I prepare breakfast, lunch, and dinner and work at the restaurant long hours to help provide and keep a clean house." Tears filled the corner of Laura's amber-colored eyes.

"Oh, so you think your job is hard? Well, how about try writing hours and hours for three years. It was my best story yet. It was sure to bring lots of money," said Winston. He paced back and forth in the bedroom. His eyebrows were low and his top lip curled up in the corners. "There is only one thing left to do," Winston uttered.

Laura stared at him like a small child dreading discipline. Her hand began to tremble as she awaited his response. The few seconds of silence caused her heart to beat faster.

"I will just have to start completely over," sighed Winston.

Laura's face dropped. "Winston, I thought … well, I was hoping we would try to start a family. It's been eight years now," she said, looking down to hide her tears.

"Children? How can you bring up children when all I can think of is my missing manuscript? You heartless nag! Where's your compassion!?" he yelled.

Winston walked away, upstairs to the guest room raging like heavy wind blowing in the air. The guest room is where he wrote—his sanctuary, his home inside the house. Many stories had been born in the guest room. Some took six months to complete. Moments later, Winston sat down, took out his pen, and began to write.

~

The next day Laura was off work. Still feeling terrible about her husband's lost manuscript, she decided to prepare an extra hearty breakfast of fried potatoes, buttered bread, large tea, bacon, and beans. *He didn't eat dinner last night. He should be very hungry right now,* she thought.

As she held the plate of food, she knocked on the heavy door. "Winston? Winston dear," she said in the sweetest voice. "I prepared a lovely breakfast for you."

"Leave it by the door," said Winston.

Laura obeyed his command but in her heart, she wanted him to greet her directly. Coming down stairs and joining her at mealtime would be ideal; nonetheless, Laura remained hopeful. Winston and Laura used to have breakfast together on her off days, but it became less and less over the years, especially as his love for writing grew more and more intense.

An hour went by. Laura wondered why Winston hadn't come downstairs to compliment her on such a wonderfully prepared meal. She tried to recall the last time she received compliments, maybe several years. Hearing any kind words would mean so much to her, especially now.

Laura walked up the stairs and when she approached the door, her eyes bulged. Winston had eaten less than half of what was on his plate. Feeling dejected, she picked up the plate from the floor, brought it to the kitchen, and put the leftovers in the insulated icebox.

Maybe he'll eat more for lunch, she thought.

Another hour later, Laura prepared a lunch of sliced meat, pudding, a biscuit, and a small fruit. She placed his food on a tray and carried it upstairs.

"Winston, Winston dear. I prepared a wonderful lunch," she said. She eagerly awaited his response, hoping he would come out and acknowledge her.

"Leave it by the door," replied Winston.

"Yes, my love," sighed Laura.

Disappointed, Laura slowly walked downstairs, thinking of a way to get her husband to come out of the guest room. Suddenly, Laura's heart-shaped face lit up.

"Yes, that's it! I know what will work! I'll

prepare him a lovely dinner. After I cook dinner, I'll bathe and wear a nice scented perfume."

Laura was thrilled about her idea and was eager to start. She cooked everything perfectly, leaving just enough time to bathe and mist herself with a flower-scented perfume. She went upstairs feeling optimistic that her husband would welcome her at the door, become stimulated by the aroma of her sweet perfume and home-cooked delectable meal, and join her.

"Winston? Winston, dear? May I come in?"

Laura could hear heavy footsteps pound on the hardwood floor, followed by the door knob turning. Laura's heart was beating faster knowing that she would see Winston's face.

"What is it?" asked Winston, leaning next to the door still looking at a sheet of paper.

"I cooked asparagus, baked chicken and rice, and poured you a glass of white wine." She smiled, hoping he would acknowledge her the way a husband should acknowledge his wife.

"Just place it by the door," said Winston.

After Winston slammed the door, Laura stood numb for several seconds. She put her head down and tears fell to the floor.

~

For seven months things remained unchanged. Winston continued to eat, sleep, and write in the guest room while Laura continued to work long shifts at the local restaurant for five, sometimes six days a week. Laura was weary. Her lips were pale, her face was swollen, and her eyelids drooped. She felt discouraged.

~

One morning Winston looked down the stairwell and called, "Laura? Laura, where are you?"

He went downstairs and found a lovely breakfast laid out on the table. Laura was nowhere to be found. A note was propped up against his glass of fresh squeezed orange juice.

'Winston dear, I must say goodbye. I cannot continue to be in such a cruel matrimony as this. I've grown weary of being your maid and cook while your obsession with your manuscript in the guest room grows stronger and stronger. Instead of caressing me, you cuddle with your pen. Instead of kissing me, you lick your fingers for turning pages. Instead of making love to me, you choose to create beautiful words for chapters in your story. Instead of starting a family with me, you choose to bring life to another manuscript. Goodbye, Laura.'

Winston took a long deep breath, then reached for the small pitcher of still-warm maple syrup and poured it over fluffy homemade Belgian waffles. He ate voraciously, his appetite suddenly kicking in.

With a last gulp of juice, Winston got up from the table and headed upstairs to the guest room, his heart racing. Beads of sweat gathered on his forehead in anticipation as he walked toward the closet and opened it.

Inside was a medium-size box. Removing a key from his pocket, he unlocked the box and grinned.

As he reached in, a sudden sharp pain gripped his heart. He crumpled to the floor, still clutching his manuscript.

Mr. Ma'am and Ms. Sir

*P*aul arrived at a small café and ordered his usual drink. "I'd like an espresso, please."

After several minutes, the cashier yelled, "I've got one espresso!"

He reached for the drink just as another customer reached for it.

"Uh, excuse me, but I think that's my order," said Alexa.

"Are you sure, because I just placed an order for an espresso," said Paul.

The cashier intervened. "Oh, I'm sorry, Sir, but this customer's order was placed before yours. We'll have yours up shortly."

Alexa felt bad for the confusion and showed an act of kindness. "You know what? Here. You can have mine."

"No, no, I can't do that. You've been waiting here longer than I have, but I appreciate the offer."

"No, really, I insist," said Alexa.

"That's very kind of you," said Paul.

Not long after, the same cashier called out another order. "I have an order for an espresso!"

Alexa walked toward the cashier and took the drink. "Don't worry. I'm not double dipping or double drinking. I gave my espresso to that customer," she said.

She turned and noticed Paul sitting alone.

"I'm sorry to impose, but I wonder if you would like some company," asked Alexa.

"Well, it depends on what else you're offering; I'm just kidding. Please. Sit," chuckled Paul.

Alexa laughed. "You have quite a sense of humor. I like that. I'm Alexa. So do you come here often?"

"Hi. I'm Paul. I pop in here from time to time. And you?"

"Same here. I stop by periodically but never gave away my espresso. You're the first."

"Well, it's the first time that I've ever accepted anyone's espresso," replied Paul.

"Well, how about meeting back here and we can exchange espressos again … let's say Friday same time?" asked Alexa.

"You got yourself a date," said Paul.

The next several months were wonderful for Alexa and Paul. They genuinely enjoyed each other's company and looked forward to the time they spent together.

"That was such a great movie. Thank you so much for suggesting it. Next time, my treat," said Paul.

"No, no. I don't mind paying," replied Alexa.

"And I don't mind treating my sweetie either," said Paul.

"Okay, fair enough. So, something's been on my mind. Ever since I met you, I feel that I can be myself. And, I mean truly be myself. Spending time with you has been so wonderful, and I want you to meet my family. But ... there's something about me you need to know," said Alexa.

"Wow! I feel the exact same way and want you to meet my family as well. So, what is it that you need to tell me?" asked Paul.

"Well, I'm not exactly who you think I am," said Alexa.

"What do you mean?"

Well, I wasn't born as Alexa. I was born Alex."

Paul breathed a sigh of relief. "My birth name is Paula."

Puzzled By Love

"Cute cat ... look at the cat." Emma pointed to the puzzle.

"Oh, how adorable; did you give the cat a name, Ms. Emma?" asked the nurse.

Emma paused briefly. "I'll name it Kitty Kitty."

Emma's nurse looked at another nurse and quickly shook her head from side to side.

"Okay, Ms. Emma, it's time to go now. Say goodnight to William," explained the nurse.

"But I want to play with him. He's my friend," pouted Emma.

The nurse assisted Emma as she stood up. "You will play again tomorrow, Ms. Emma."

Emma waved to William as another nurse prepared to walk him back to his room. William and Emma both suffered from Alzheimer's and loved solving a variety of puzzles together, ranging from twenty to twenty-five pieces.

Emma giggled like a teenager with a big crush. "He's my friend. I like him."

"And he likes you very much too," replied the nurse as she assisted Emma back to her room.

"I want to play puzzle with him. I like him," said Emma.

The nurse helped Emma prepare for bed. "You will play puzzle again next time after you get a good night's sleep."

Emma smiled and slowly dozed off. "I like him."

~

Later in the evening, the two nurses chatted.

"That Ms. Emma is something else," said the second nurse.

"Yes, she sure is; love her to death. Can't believe she never married and has no kids," replied Emma's nurse.

The next morning, Emma's nurse received a package. Inside, it contained a note. It was from Emma's niece, Ms. Ritchie.

Hi. Before my mom passed, she told me that Aunt Emma always had this fascination with Paris. I think this puzzle might help my aunt. Hopefully her friend can help her solve it as there are more pieces included than they are used to working on. Please keep me posted on the results. In the meantime, I'll continue looking for more puzzles. Thank you so much for all your help. Sincerely, Alice Ritchie.

Emma's nurse held the note against her heart and smiled. "Oh, this is wonderful! I can't wait to show this to Ms. Emma."

Emma's afternoon was filled with fun activities. She played bingo with other patients, but putting together puzzles with William seemed to be her favorite.

"Okay, Ms. Emma, it's time to do puzzles with your friend, William," explained the nurse.

"I'm going to see my friend now," Emma said to the nurse.

The nurse assisted Emma to a round wooden table that she and William often worked on. "Yes, that's right, Ms. Emma, you and William are going to work on a puzzle now."

Emma and William waited quietly at the table. Thirty-six large puzzles pieces were in front of them. Seconds later, Emma laughed out loud, prompting her nurse to sit by her side.

Emma handed William one piece at a time. Soon she and William had put together several pieces.

Almost an hour later, they made it to their last piece. William allowed Emma to place the final piece in the puzzle. He paused for a few seconds, followed by tears of joy. Suddenly, Emma began crying. William clutched her hands and they cried and laughed together.

Later that evening, Emma's nurse called Emma's niece. "Ms. Ritchie. I'm sorry to call you so late, but something wonderful happened tonight! That Eiffel Tower puzzle you sent did something because Miss Emma and the other patient burst into tears after finishing it. We don't know what could have possibly brought them both to tears."

Ms. Ritchie shrieked. "Oh! Is everything alright?"

"Yes, yes, they're fine. These were happy tears. They started crying and laughing … and held each other's hands," exclaimed the nurse.

"Oh my goodness, I can't believe this! I was going to call you tomorrow morning, but I'm glad we're able to speak now. I found one of my aunt's storage boxes and came across an old picture of her, along with a few other people, standing in front of the Eiffel Tower in Paris. On the back of the picture are some names: *Talinda, James, Emma, and my love, Willie*."

Sliding In Love

"**9**-1-1; for what city?"

"I'm in Madison Park."

Do you require police, fire, or ambulance?"

"I need an ambulance."

What's the address of the emergency?"

"I'm at Land's Park Trail."

As she stared at her bloody leg, Marianne remained calm.

"Tell me what happened."

Marianne gave her name and said, "While I was riding my mountain bike down a hill I tripped over some sticks. A piece of the wood pierced my leg."

"When did this happen?"

"Just a few minutes before calling 9-1-1, around 10:15 a.m."

"Okay, I'm sending the paramedics to help

you now."

Marianne released a faint moan. "Thank you."

She felt relieved that help was on the way. She called her parents, who lived four hours away, and gave them updates.

"Yes, I'm in a lot of pain, Pops, but I'll be fine. Let Mom know I'll be alright. Gotta hang up now. The paramedics are on their way. I'll call you back once I get to the hospital. Love you," said Marianne.

As the ambulance pulled up, the pain from her leg became more intense. A lean male who appeared to be about 6'0 in height stepped out of the emergency vehicle and approached her.

"Hi. Are you Marianne Evans?"

"Yes."

"I'm Thomas. I'm a paramedic. We're gonna get you checked out, okay? I want you to relax and try not to move your leg for me."

Marianne couldn't help but notice the peaceful vibe that exuded from the paramedic along with the dimples perfectly placed on his chiseled face.

As the emergency driver rolled out a gurney, Thomas performed a complete assessment. "We're going to transfer you very carefully into the ambulance now."

Once inside the medical vehicle, Marianne

glanced at what appeared to be a 'hospital in a van.' She looked dumbfounded. "Wow. So this is what the inside looks like."

"Your first time inside one of these, huh? Well, we want to make sure there won't be a second time," said Thomas.

Marianne's curiosity was sparked. "I bet you see a lot of accidents in your line of work." She pointed to her leg. "Anything like this ...?"

"Oh, I've seen worse, but I love helping people. Hearing the call about a woman being injured from sliding down a hill was a reminder that I picked the right career," Thomas said as he checked her vitals.

Marianne looked puzzled. "How is that?"

"When my younger brother and I were kids, we loved riding our bikes. My brother ended up sliding down a hill and falling off his bike, injuring himself. That was the day I knew I wanted to help people," explained Thomas.

"Is it just you and your brother? Do you have other siblings?"

"I have an older sister. How about you?"

"No, I'm an only child," replied Marianne.

Thomas continued checking her vitals. "Must have been pretty lonely."

"Yeah. It wasn't always easy finding friends."

"Ah. I know the feeling. I loved playing on the slides at school when I was a kid, but I was teased by a classmate, so I tried to avoid the play area as much as possible. She picked on me all the time," Thomas explained.

"I think it was her way of showing you that she liked you. And you were lucky. My family was military, so we moved a lot. I hated it. It was another reason why it was hard to make friends," said Marianne.

"Sounds like we both shared something in common as kids—finding friends."

The conversation helped Marianne take her mind off the pain.

"So tell me how long have you been bike riding?" asked Thomas.

"For a few weeks now … I like to find new locations once in a while. But I love it here."

"I can definitely see why. The scenery is beautiful."

"You ride? You should visit," said Marianne.

"You know, I think I will. Well, it looks like we've arrived," said Thomas.

Thomas and the other the medical driver rolled Marianne out of the vehicle and entered the hospital.

After speaking with one of the medical staff, Thomas, smiling, turned to Marianne. "Okay, they're going to take really good care of you and get you all patched up. Should be a quick recovery. Maybe we'll run into each other on that bike path once you're healed."

"Look forward to it," replied Marianne.

For Marianne, a few hours in the hospital felt like months. Being confined to a hospital bed was something she was unaccustomed to.

A nurse walked in her room with release forms. "Hi there, how are you feeling?"

"Feeling ready to get home. Just waiting for my ride," replied Marianne.

The nurse chuckled. "You'll be there shortly."

"Seriously, everyone here has been wonderful. He wasn't kidding when he said I would be in good hands. He was really cool."

"Who is that, ma'am?" asked the nurse.

"The paramedic who brought me in."

"Oh, I see," replied the nurse.

The nurse continued reviewing the release forms.

"You know, he told me he was picked on in school. When I was in school, I remember this kid who always passed gas whenever going down the slides. I used to call him Art Fart. I was military and moved a lot so I didn't know him very well, not even his last name. I guess it was my mean way of saying that I liked him. For a minute, I thought the same boy could have been the paramedic," said Marianne.

"That poor kid; why did you call him Art Fart?" asked the nurse.

"Well, his first name was Arthur. Get it?" asked Marianne.

The nursed glanced at Marianne. "Wait a minute; the paramedic who helped you, was his name Thomas?"

Marianne looked confused. "Yeah; why?

The nurse paused. "Because he always addresses himself by his last name. His first name is Arthur."

.

Thank You, Officer

*W*hat is taking her so long? I told her we were leaving at 7:00. I can't be late.

As Kellie sat in her car, her lips tightened. She blew the horn a few times. Seconds later, her younger sister walked out of a modern looking house and ran toward an old Honda.

Kellie looked irritated and rolled her eyes. "It took you long enough. I told you that I needed to leave by 7:00. Trying to find a parking spot downtown is a pain."

"Sorry, Sis ... couldn't find my other shirt," replied Kellie's sister.

"Okay, let's just hurry up and get you to school so I can get to work on time."

"Thanks for giving me a ride. Um ... can you give me a ride tomorrow? I think my friend's car will be fixed later today, but asking ... just in case."

Kellie sighed. "Yeah, just be on time."

"I wish all big sisters were like you!"

Kellie gave a soft smile. "Yeah, yeah, just please be on time."

The idea of taking her sister to school all week annoyed Kelli but she distinctly remembered those days in high school, walking to school in that heat and bumming rides with any of her friends who had cars. Nonetheless, her sister's comment touched her heart. She felt good knowing she was able to help out her younger sister.

Kellie pulled to the curve in front of the school. "Okay, see you later."

Kellie's sister jumped out of the car. "Thanks, sis; later!"

I should get there by 7:45. That's not too bad.

Kellie pulled out of the parking lot and scanned the area to make sure there were no students in sight or police officers hiding out. The fastest way to get her destination would require a U-turn. Kellie was hesitant at first but the thought of being late for work did not sit well with her.

As she waited at the light, she glanced around for a second time, making sure there were no cops or kids around.

I'll drive a little faster. It should be okay. Besides,

school's already started.

The light turned green; Kellie was four vehicles behind. The vehicle in front of her hesitated.

What? You gotta be kidding me! What is the driver doing?

Annoyed, Kellie blew the horn twice. After several seconds, the driver in front of her finally moved as the traffic light switched to red. Kellie busted a U-turn anyway, ditched the 25 mph speed limit, and increased close to 35 mph.

After Kelli completed the turn, she was startled by the sound of a police siren coming from behind.

No, No, No! Where in the world did he come from? I didn't see any police around.

Kellie pulled over, rolled down her windows, and searched for her license and registration. She felt sick as she was not only going to be late, but would receive her first ticket, a harsh one to be exact.

Oh shoot, here he comes, and he looks mean, too. Great.

"Good morning, ma'am. Do you know why you're being pulled over?" asked the policeman.

"Good morning, Officer. I know I made that illegal turn. I'm sorry, Officer, but the driver in front of me caused me to miss the light, and my sister was running late, which caused me to be running late for work. I'm just trying to get to work on time."

"Ma'am, I also clocked you going 35 in a 25 mph. I'll need your registration, license, and insurance."

Kellie had all of the documents except for her insurance card.

Oh crap.

Kellie searched through her compartment. "I'm going to look in here again, but I think I left my insurance card at home. I just renewed it and forgot to put it in my car."

"Okay, ma'am. Sit tight."

Kellie rested her elbow on the window frame and rested her head on her fingers.

So we're looking at an illegal U-turn, speeding, and no insurance card. That's three strikes ... I'm out. I despise baseball right about now. Only a miracle can get me out of this ticket.

Kellie's anxiety level increased every minute. She stared through the rearview mirror waiting for the officer to return.

Oh no, here he comes. Here we go.

The officer approached Kellie and handed back her forms. "Ma'am, your insurance card was verified so you're good, but make sure you keep it with you in the car at all times."

Kellie felt some relief but was more concerned about receiving a ticket for the speeding and the illegal turn.

"I'm giving you a warning this time, but please make sure you follow the traffic rules and use caution on the road," said the officer.

Kellie felt as though she had stepped into an episode of *The Twilight Zone* or was secretly being filmed for the next episode of *What Would You Do* television show.

"Drive safe, ma'am," said the policeman.

Kellie was mystified. "Thank you, Officer." Still in shock from not getting a ticket, and also in a rush to get to work, she stepped on the gas, not realizing she had put the car in reverse.

Kellie heard a loud thump and looked in the rearview mirror. She saw the driver step out of the damaged vehicle and approach her car. She took a deep breath, rolled down her window and said, "Hello again, Officer."

The Complicated Couple

"Good morning," Don said as he made coffee. "So, last night was pretty good, considering it was our first night."

"Yeah, I thought so too," replied Tori.

Don poured coffee into a travel mug. "I'll do my best to put in more effort. So how about we do it again this evening after dinner?"

"Well, the doctor did say a few times per week is best, so I think we should, but not so gentle this time. As for dinner … we can have that leftover spaghetti you cooked a couple of nights ago," said Tori.

Don grabbed his briefcase from the counter and headed toward the door. "Well, there wasn't much spaghetti left, so I packed it for lunch today. Whatever you want to eat tonight is fine with me."

"Okay, I'll grab something on my way home

from work," said Tori.

"Well, I better get going." Don kissed Tori on the cheek. "Have a great day."

Tori smiled and watched Don head to the door. "Thanks. Hope you have a good day, too."

Tori typically left for work about a half hour after her husband headed out to his job. Normally, he left crumbs on the table and she had to wipe them from the counters and put everything back in its place, but surprisingly, the kitchen was spotless. It looked just like how she left it from the night before.

Don arrived home by 5:30 p.m., his usual time, and did his daily after work routine, consisting of eating a snack, sitting on a leather recliner, taking off his shoes, and closing his eyes while tears rolled down his face. But tonight was different. There were no tears. He grabbed a book and began reading. Before getting to the third chapter, he was suddenly jolted by the sound of his wife entering their home.

Tori walked in the front door carrying a laptop and a bag of takeout. She placed her keys on a stand in the foyer and walked into the living room.

Don greeted her warmly. "How was your day?"

"It was fine. How was yours?" Tori glanced

at the coffee table where she would normally find one or two crumpled tissues, but tonight, she didn't find any.

"Not too bad." He stared at the takeout bag. "So, we're having Chinese?"

"Yes. I know we had it a couple of times already this week, but it's the closest restaurant. Is that okay?" she asked.

"Uh, sure," he replied.

When they sat down to eat, Tori confessed, "I appreciate what you did this morning. The kitchen looked so nice and clean."

Don gave a warm grin and his tone was happy. "You're welcome."

"So my parents are throwing a BBQ cookout next Sunday. I told them we'll be there."

Don's voice suddenly turned somewhat less enthusiastic. "Oh, okay. It was a nice visit last weekend ... and the weekend before that."

Several minutes passed. Don and Tori were silent as they ate the last bite of Kung Pao Chicken.

"So, we agreed to do it again tonight. Are you ready?" asked Don.

"I'm ready," Tori replied.

The next morning started off wonderfully. Tori met Don in the kitchen enthusiastically, and everything appeared to be clean like the day before.

"Good morning, Dear," said Don.

"Good morning, Honey. Last night was so good … and I have a surprise for you later."

Don gave Tori a curious glance. "A surprise?"

"Yep, but you have to wait about ten or so more hours to find out. Have a great day at work," explained Tori.

Later that evening, Tori arrived home almost two hours before Don and prepared a lovely home-cooked meal consisting of two small T-Bone steaks, shrimp scampi, scalloped potatoes, and oven-roasted vegetables. Just as she finished preparing, she heard the sound of the garage door opening.

When Don walked through the door he sniffed the air and went directly into the kitchen. "Aw, this smells so good!" He glanced at the beautifully prepared food. "Oh, wow, this looks amazing."

"Well, after last night, I thought I'd make a special dinner," said Tori.

"So this was the surprise you had for me?"

"Hmm, part of it; I'll share the other half after we eat," replied Tori.

"Can't wait. By the way, I picked up a lemon pie."

Tori's eyes widened. "You did? Thank you, Honey."

They sat down and began eating. Their conversation was slightly different tonight, as they both appeared more relaxed and playful.

Tori wiped her mouth with a napkin. "That was really good."

"It was better than good; it was amazing. Thanks for working hard preparing all of this," said Don.

Tori looked like a teenage girl with a crush. "You're welcome. I think I want some of that lemon pie. Do you want some?"

"Yeah, I'll try a little bit. You know, those jeans look really great on you," said Don.

Tori beamed. "Thanks."

She cut two small pieces of pie, gave a slice to her husband, and then both began eating.

"So, are you ready for the other surprise?" asked Tori.

Don took the last bite of the pie and wiped his mouth with a napkin. "Of course, I am."

"Well, today at work, I told my boss that I can't continue working overtime and agreed to stay only one day a week instead of five, starting Monday. Also … I told my parents we won't be visiting next weekend," said Tori.

Don and Tori grinned shyly at each other.

"You want to go for a third night?" asked Don.

Tori glowed. "Yeah."

~

Two days later, Don and Tori arrived at their Saturday appointment. A staff assistant opened a door and greeted them. "Hi there, come on back. Dr. Peterson will see you now."

A tall older woman greeted the couple. "Well, hello there. Please have a seat. So tell me, you two, how are things coming along?"

"It's going amazing, actually," said Tori.

"Yeah, much better than we expected," said Don.

"I'm noticing a big improvement in your body language. I'm glad to see that you both agreed to use this method to express your desires and needs with each other. Sharing your feelings and thoughts, especially in a marriage, is critical, and as you can see, it doesn't always have to be accomplished in the most common way," replied the doctor.

"So should we continue doing what we've been doing?" asked Tori.

"Yes, absolutely. I'd suggest at least two or three nights for another week. It will continue to encourage the growth of intimacy," replied the doctor.

Later that evening, Don and Tori prepared a tasty home-cooked meal together and shared a friendly conversation.

"That was delicious, Dear. You know, I think we're pretty creative together in the kitchen," said Don.

Tori smiled. "Yes, we are, huh? But I think we can be even more creative somewhere else."

He paused for a moment and then expressed his excitement. "You know, we covered food and cooking, work schedules, cleaning, money, and quality time, but I don't think we ever included romance in our nightly routine."

Tori agreed. "And the doctor did say we should continue for at least another week."

"I'm ready if you are," grinned Don.

They both stood up and went to change clothes. A few minutes later they met in the living room, pushed back the sofa and coffee table, and slipped on their boxing gloves.

.

The Dream

"**O**kay, Ladies and Gentlemen, a reminder, your theses are due tomorrow afternoon. And please be on time for my lecture," stated Professor Mack.

The graduate students gathered their belongings and walked out of the auditorium. Professor Mack hurried behind, hoping to get to an appointment on time.

As she approached her car, she heard the familiar voice of a colleague heading her way.

"Professor Mack! Hi. Do you have a minute?"

"Yes, of course, Dr. Hughes, but only a minute. How can I help you?"

"Would you be available to speak at the academic conference next week?"

"I'd love to, but I'll have to check my schedule," she replied.

"Great, I'll send you an email with more info.

Thank you!" Professor Hughes smiled and waved goodbye.

Professor Mack unlocked her car door, slid in and placed her laptop on the front passenger seat, and started the engine. As she pulled out of her parking spot, she saw one of her students, Sean, throwing a football to another student.

In the blink of an eye, screams were heard from nearby pedestrians, catching the professor's attention.

Suddenly, out of nowhere a vehicle came speeding around the corner leaving Sean crumpled on the pavement.

Professor Mack put her car in park, trembling from having witnessed the horrible scene.

As people gathered around, Professor Mack didn't move, too nervous to get out of her car. She was afraid of what she might see, but she wanted to make sure Sean was okay.

She finally stepped out and darted toward the crowd, but at only 5'3", it was difficult to get a good view. Then a voice shouted, "He's pretty banged up; call 911!"

~

BEEP BEEP, BEEP BEEP, BEEP BEEP. The sound of the alarm jolted Professor Mack awake. She rubbed her hands over her face.

"Wow. That was an awful dream."

An hour later, Professor Mack was dressed and ready to head out the door. The same tremble she had in her dream suddenly felt real. As she drove to the university, the accident kept flashing through her mind. The frequent quivers increased when she parked.

Another professor greeted her. "Good morning, Dr. Mack. Are you okay? You seem a bit jittery this morning."

"Yes, I'm fine—no wait, I'm not okay, actually. Let me ask you a question. What do you know about dreams?" she asked.

"Well, my area of expertise is accounting, so you may want to reach out to Professor Sanders in the Psychology Department. But generally speaking, I think dreams are all about the person who is having them," said the other professor.

"So, you're saying that other people in our dreams do not have any significance?" asked Professor Mack.

"I suppose. I mean, I once had a dream that a handsome movie star swept me off my feet. Guess what? No one has knocked on my door holding a broom," replied the professor.

They chuckled and walked into the building.

Professor Mack arrived in the auditorium,

took out lecture materials, and prepared for a presentation. Her brief conversation with her colleague put her mind at ease, although she was still eager to see Sean, who was enrolled in her class that morning.

As students entered the building, they chatted with one another. As Professor Mack approached the podium, she glanced up and breathed a sigh of relief when she saw Sean sitting with the others.

The professor thought, *Yep, it was just a dream ... a silly dream.*

An Hour Later

"Okay, Ladies and Gentlemen, I hope you all enjoyed today's lecture. Now, it's time to hand in those amazing papers that I'm absolutely looking forward to reading."

Professor Mack watched as the students paraded up to the podium one by one, with Sean among the last. He handed her his paper, smiled and said, "See you Thursday."

She piled all the papers into her briefcase and exited the lecture hall. She heard her name being called as she headed toward the parking lot.

"Dr. Mack! Hi. Do you have a minute?"

"Yes, of course, Dr. Hughes, but only a minute. I need to get to an appointment. How can I help you?" asked the professor.

"Would you be available to speak at the academic conference next week?"

Professor Mack paused, a weird feeling of deja vu recalling her dream. "I'd love to, but I need to check my schedule."

"Great, I'll send you an email with more information. Thank you!" Professor Hughes waved goodbye.

Professor Mack was baffled, but continued walking to her car. As she reached the parking lot, she caught a glimpse of Sean throwing a football.

The Honest Hat Snatcher

Old Man Cramer sat on the wooden bench at a big park. He was quite tired from walking. He watched young people playing volleyball, then decided to go for one more walk seeing that the park wasn't very crowded.

After completing his second round, Old Man Cramer returned and found a hat on the bench. He sat down for a brief minute, placing his book next to him. Then he put on his reading glasses, took a closer look at the hat, and walked away with it, flashing a huge grin.

Several minutes later, a young man approached the bench and discovered the hat was missing. He looked around the park and from a distance saw the old man holding the hat and getting onto a transit bus.

"Hey, my hat … that old man stole my hat!" yelled the young man.

A Great Day for Ice Cream

It was too late to stop the old man. The bus drove away. Then the young man noticed a book on the bench. He opened it up and looked inside, hoping to find any information on the elderly man. The only thing he discovered was what appeared to be a medical prescription receipt. He took the information to the police station and filed a report.

~

Old Man Cramer was in a jolly mood. He felt satisfied as he stared at his collection of hats.

His mood was interrupted by several knocks on his door. "This is the Metropolitan Police."

Old Man Cramer looked through the peep hole and saw two police officers standing at his doorstep. *What in the world is going on?* He opened the door and said, "Yes, officers ... how may I help you gentlemen?"

"Mr. Michael Cramer?" asked the first officer.

"Why yes, Sir, that's me. Michael Cramer," said the old man.

"May we come in, Sir?" asked the second officer.

"Why yes, please come in," said the old man.

"Well, we have a report that you took a hat at the park around 2:30 p.m. this afternoon. Is this correct, Sir?" asked the first officer.

"Why yes, sir, I sure did. I snatched it up as soon as I saw it," said the old man.

"So you admit to taking the hat?" asked the first officer.

"Why, of course, and I would do it again if I had to," said the old man.

"Say what?" The first police officer looked quite puzzled.

"Well, you see, it's a one-of-a-kind and very valuable," said the old man.

"So you mean to tell me that you admit to taking the hat and that you would do it again if you had to?" asked the first police officer.

"That's exactly what I said, Officer. You see, I've been walking that park every day for the last couple of weeks waiting to get that hat. Just think, had I not shown up today, I probably would have never gotten my hands on it," said the old man.

"Sir, you do know that robbery is a crime?" The officer looked around his house. "You've got quite a hat collection here. Can you show us the hat you took yesterday?"

"Robbery? Why, I've done no such thing," said the old man. He walked to a table stand, picked up the hat, and brought it to the officer.

The first police officer closely examined the hat while the second officer glanced at a picture on the wall.

The second officer looked shocked. "Hey, he's wearing the same hat in this picture."

"Well, I'll be ..." swore the first police officer. Inside, he found a year and small name engraved that read: *1970, Michael Cramer*.

The Joker's Gift

"Hey sir, can I wash your windows today?" asked a solicitor.

"No. I'm good," Simon replied as he walked into a two-story building.

"Good morning, Simon. Did you get the message from a Mr. Modine? He said he's been trying to reach you," said an assistant secretary.

Simon snatched the sticky note from the secretary. "Of course he has, along with every other author on the planet."

Once he arrived in his office, it didn't take Simon long to get situated. He was very orderly and took his profession as a book critic seriously.

He picked up his office phone and dialed. "This is Simon Trent. Is this Patrick Modine?"

"Yes. Hello, Mr. Trent. I'm happy to finally connect with you, Sir. So, I'm in need of a book critic for the first trilogy of my novel series, *The*

Whispering Dawn. It's a combination of various genres that's not considered a popular mix, but I consider myself to be a visionary writer. I've paused on publishing until after getting it critiqued," replied Patrick.

"Well, Mr. Modine, I'm sorry, but I already have a stack of books waiting to be critiqued. I could drop some names of other critics who could help you," replied Simon.

"I appreciate that, but I wouldn't have reached out to you if I wanted another critic. I know your work, and you're one of the best critics out there; besides, it took me eight years to complete this epic novel, so patience is one of my virtues," replied the man.

Simon took another look at his calendar. "Okay, I can have it completed in six months."

After the two men ended the conversation, Simon told himself. *This better be worth my time.*

~

Simon made it through a five hundred page novel and was able to critique Modine's book sooner than expected. He found the novel to be well written, but he had mixed feelings about the multiple genres and didn't believe it would grab the audience. Despite his distaste, he gave the author a decent critique.

Three Weeks Later

Simon was at his desk reading an article online and was interrupted by the secretary's knock on his door. "Sorry to bother, but you've got a package from Patrick Modine."

"Open it, please," asked Simon.

"It looks like a first edition of *The Whispering Dawn*." The secretary handed it to Simon.

Simon expressed little interest. He placed the book back in the package, as he had no desire or plans to keep it, and decided to return it.

When he stepped out the building and headed to lunch, he became irritated at the same young car washer who approached him.

"Hey, want your windows washed today?"

"No, I don't need my windows washed today or any other day for that matter." Simon stopped and looked grudgingly at the washer who appeared to be about nineteen- or twenty-years-old. "You ever thought about getting a real job?"

"This is my job. I'm gonna save up a lot of money and one day open a car wash business, lots of them, all over town," replied the young man.

Simon thought, *Wow, this poor guy is completely delusional*. He looked at the package Patrick gave him, pulled out the book, and handed it to the young window washer. "Here ... take this. It's a fantasy book. I think you'll find more enjoyment out of it than I will ... and good luck with that car wash business."

The young man was surprised. "Wow, thanks, Mister. I never got a gift from anybody."

One Year Later

Working from his desk, Simon suddenly grunted and dropped a book on his desk.

Don't people know anything about writing a great novel these days? What happened to style and pacing?

The secretary rushed in Simon's office. "Did you hear the news?"

"I've been busy, so you'll have to tell me," snapped Simon.

"*The Whispering Dawn* trilogy just hit record-breaking sales. There's talk of it being adapted into a major television series. It could possibly surpass *Seinfeld's* record of most successful shows of all time!" exclaimed the staff worker.

Simon's eyes enlarged. "What! It was well written but ... but I'd never ... there is no way possible it could have ever reached this level."

"Well, apparently, someone disagreed, or more like millions of someones disagreed. Lucky for you—you have the first edition. A book like that is priceless."

The Last Lottery Ticket

"So, what would you do if you won the jackpot?" the news anchorwoman asked.

Ed walked past a middle-aged looking couple being interviewed. He grinned as he overheard the woman telling all the many things she would do.

Ed took out his wallet and slipped the cashier ten bucks. "How's it going? It's pretty crazy out there with those lines," said Ed.

"Hey, how you been; haven't seen you in a while. Any luck on the game when the jackpot was up to four hundred million? Hard to believe that was just three months ago," said the cashier.

"Well, not the big one, that's for sure I'll take a couple of quick picks," said Ed.

"Maybe you'll be the lucky winner for this one. Good luck." The cashier handed Ed his tickets and change.

"Don't need luck. I'm getting those matching numbers." Ed waved goodbye.

The next morning, Ed was awakened by the excitement of his sister's voice.

"Ed! Ed! Somebody hit. Someone hit ... right here in Okerton Valley!"

"You got to be kidding me! I told that cashier I was getting those matching numbers. But don't even think about yelling them out. You know I like waiting until the last day."

"I know you like waiting to the last minute and all, but someone in our town hit! When was the last time that ever happened ... like ... never!" shouted Ed's sister.

"Sis, trust me, I've got those numbers, but I'm still going to wait to make sure no one else comes forward. That will confirm it. Now, I think I'll leave a little bit early for work today." Ed smiled and headed to the kitchen as his sister glared, holding her hips.

Three months later and still no one had come forward to claim the billion dollar ticket. Ed stuck to his word, despite his sister's subtle tactics. She desperately wanted him to check his numbers. One day over dinner, she told the story of a lottery winner who missed out on his winnings all because he wanted to search for a reputable tax accountant and ended up misplacing his ticket before the deadline. Nonetheless, the story did not faze Ed one bit.

Later that night, Ed was in such a fantastic mood, he prepared dinner.

"Hey, Sis, I made your favorite: homemade lemon butter chicken pasta."

"Oh yum … thank you, thank you! You know, I can seriously get used to this, especially after a long day at work." She noticed that Ed's smile seemed to be wider. "Okay, you're smiling and I mean big. Did you check your numbers?"

"Of course not; I'm smiling because I'll be finally moving out sooner than I expected. Getting my own place, so you two love birds can live like newlyweds," Ed said while placing two plates of pasta on the table.

"Well, I can see why you would be happy about that. But it's been pretty nice having you around, especially since Chris has been working night shifts at the hospital the last couple of weeks," Ed's sister said.

After giving thanks for the food, she cleverly attempted to bring up another tragic story of how a lotto winner missed out. "You know, Ed, I read an interesting article today regarding ways to invest lottery winnings …"

Ed cut her off.

"Okay, Sis, I know where this conversation is going. I'm not checking my numbers and that's that, so let's just sit and enjoy this wonderful home-cooked meal prepared by your wonderful baby brother."

"Alright … fine. Hand me the pepper," said his sister.

Five months and two weeks passed and the winning ticket was still unclaimed. With only fourteen days remaining, Ed had no doubt in his mind that he had the matching numbers. He walked down the spiral stairs to have dinner with his sister. She never raised the question again. She only hoped that her brother was the winner of the billion dollar jackpot.

The morning of the last day to claim finally arrived. Ed decided to check the winning numbers on his phone. He pulled out all the tickets in his folder and—sure enough—his numbers matched. Ed called his sister to confirm the winning numbers. She called out the numbers; they were identical to the numbers on his ticket.

Ed tried to contain his emotions but failed. He started shouting and running around the house like a maniac. "I knew I had the matching numbers. I just knew it! This is so unbelievable!"

Ed immediately got on the phone and told his boss he was not coming in to work that day. As a matter of fact, while he had his boss on the line, Ed resigned. He abruptly chose to run a few errands, the first one being a drive to a luxury dealer where he leased a Jaguar F-Type. Afterwards, he stopped by the barber to get a haircut, slipping the barber an extra tip. For his last stop, he made a quick run to the mall and bought a pair of fancy shirts totaling a few hundred dollars.

When Ed arrived back at the house, he got a call from his sister.

"Ed? I've been trying to reach you for hours. Where are you? Did you go down to claim your ticket?" she asked.

"Relax. Had to take care of a few things … besides, I still have another three hours to claim my ticket. I'm heading out right now," said Ed.

Ed stepped out the door smelling like a billion bucks. He knew the media would be camped out and he wanted to make a good impression, so he threw on his new Burberry shirt and drove his new expensive car. Ed was so impressed with the speed on his new ride, he was clueless to the noise of the police sirens behind him.

"Oh crap," sighed Ed, and pulled over to the side of the road.

"Hi, Sir, you do know you were going about 100 miles in a 50-mile zone. I need your license and registration, Sir." The officer walked away with Ed's information and returned a few minutes later. "Where were you going in such a hurry?" asked the officer.

"Well, you're not going to believe this, but I'm the one who won that billion dollar jackpot," Ed smirked, thinking the officer would let him off the hook.

"Oh really ... wow! Well, congratulations! That will definitely cover this big speeding ticket. Have a nice day, Sir." The officer handing Ed a ticket.

Ed finally arrived at the lotto store. As he pulled in closer, he saw several news reporters. He stepped out of his white Jaguar and walked into the store.

"Well, I did it. I finally hit the jackpot," smiled Ed, handing the clerk his ticket.

"Wow!" The clerk continued to examine Ed's ticket. "This is incredible. I've never seen anything like this before!"

"Yeah ... tell me about it. Nothing like waiting until the last minute. Hard to believe I'm a billionaire!" exclaimed Ed.

"Well, that's not exactly what I mean. You see, you did not win the one billion dollar lottery. The winner came forward not too long ago, but great news ... you won $100 on this ticket!" shouted the clerk.

"What! What do you mean I didn't win the billion? The numbers are right here." Ed pointed to the ticket.

"Yes, those are the right numbers, but unfortunately ... not the right game."

The Lucky Omelet

"Good afternoon, Sir. Welcome to the Dunch Café. How many in your party?"

"Just one, thank you," Fred says to the hostess.

"It's going to be about a forty-five minute wait. Is that okay? Or you can dine at the bar section, but there may be a wait there as well."

"Forty-five minutes? It's usually about fifteen. Well, I'm certainly not going to drive fifteen miles to another restaurant," replies Fred. His words are tinged with cynicism, but his tone is calm.

"I'm sorry, Sir. It's because of our unlimited soup and salad special. We've been slammed since 10:30 this morning. Here's a beeper. We'll buzz you when we have an available table."

The idea of waiting longer causes Fred's stomach to growl like a lion in the wilderness, but he decides to stay. He sits in the lobby on a leather seat, long enough to accommodate at least a dozen or more customers. Twenty-five minutes later, Fred feels his right hand tremble from the beeper's vibration.

"Well, twenty-five minutes was still a bit of a wait but certainly better than forty-five," mumbles Fred.

"This way, Sir. Your server will be right with you," explains the hostess.

Fred takes off his tan fleece-lined jacket and places it on the cherry oak chair. He looks around the wide-open restaurant as if he's never been there before. But it's not the timber décor that catches his eyes; it's the unusual number of people dining, which is a lot more than he prefers.

"Hi there, I'm Sylvia! I'll be your server today. Can I start you off with something to drink?" the bubbly server asks while placing a menu on the table.

"Well, for starters, you can take back your menu. I'll have the omelet with Jack cheddar, mushrooms, broccoli, onions, and red bell pepper with orange juice and a glass of water. Thank you," Fred says bluntly.

"Perfect. Is there anything else I can get you?"

"No, that will be it."

"Alright then, I'll go place your order." The waitress returns with a glass of water and places it on the table.

As he waits for his omelet, Fred is getting annoyed with the noise level in the restaurant. Finally, the waitress arrives with a large plate and places it on the table. He looks down at the plate, then back up at the waitress, confused and frustrated. "Uh, Miss, I asked for an omelet, not scrambled eggs and sausage," he utters.

"Oh, no, I'm so sorry about that, Sir. I'll get your order out right away!" As the waitress grabs the plate, she knocks over his glass of water, luckily less than half full at this point. "Oh, Sir, I feel so bad! This is not a good way to start my first day."

"Incredible ... I waited almost twenty-five minutes to be seated, received the wrong order, and had water spilled on me ... hmm, I'd say that everything is going quite smoothly." Fred's voice is still calm. "Just get my order, please."

In a few minutes the waitress returns with Fred's omelet. "Here you go, Sir. I explained what happened to the manager, and we're not going to charge you for the omelet," she says.

"Greatly appreciate it. Thank you," says Fred. He gives thanks for his omelet, uses his fork to cut a two-inch piece, and places it in his mouth. His eyes roll back into his head with delight as he chews. The muscles in his face move like dancing waves as he savors every bite. Fred is more than content with his omelet.

When the server stops by Fred's table, she asks, "How was it?"

"It was all worth it."

"Oh, I'm relieved and happy to hear," she says. She walks over to check on another table.

Fred stands up, puts on his jacket, pulls out money from a jacket pocket, and leaves it on the table under his plate.

As Fred is walking away the waitress catches him and wishes him a great day. She heads back to his table to clear off his plate and screams, then quickly covers her mouth with her hand.

"Are you okay? What happened?" another worker asks.

"That customer who just left gave me a $500 tip," she whispers.

"Whoa, that must have been some order. What did he have?"

"Just an omelet."

The Other Woman

"*I*'m going to call her and give her piece of my mind," said Pam.

"Hello? Hello? Who is this?" a female asked.

"You know exactly who this is! Get your own damn man and leave mine alone!" Pam yelled into the phone.

"I feel so sorry for you. Don't you understand he doesn't love you? He told me everything. I know everything about you. Once he's back from his business trip, he'll be right back here with me," said the female voice on the other end of the line.

"You're wrong! He'll never be with you. He loves me! Now you stay away from us!" Pam slammed down the phone. *She's ruining everything. I'm so sick and tired of this homewrecker.* Pam paced across the living room in the two-story condo and then dialed another number.

"Look, I just called her and told her to stay away from us. It was horrible! She said she felt sorry for me. I thought you said it was over. You told me it was over," Pam cried.

"What? What are talking about and why on are earth are you calling her? Do you not understand? You're making things worse. First ... and I'll say this the last time ... WE ARE OVER. Second, do not ever call her again. Lastly, you should make another appointment to go see your doctor. This is getting out of control," said a male voice.

"Oh, *I'm* making things worse? Fine." Pam hung up.

A few minutes later, she hit the redial and after several rings got his voice mail. Pam left a message.

"I'm sorry, babe. I'm just protecting us. I don't want this other woman to destroy what we have. I love you. Please hurry home," Pam said and dozed off to sleep.

Pam awakened the next morning feeling fatigued from the tossing and turning all night. All she could think about was the horrible conversation with the other woman. Oh how Pam wished she would just go away.

She picked up the phone, made a call, and left another voice message. "Babe, I miss you.

Where are you?" she asked.

Two hours later, Pam left another message, followed by a fourth an hour later. She thought, *Why is he not answering me?*

Later that evening, Pam made several more calls but nothing. She started to wonder if he was with the other woman. She called again but this time, instead of hearing the usual rings, it went directly to his voice mail. Pam went into a silent rage.

The next morning, Pam got out of her car and stormed into an office. "I need to see Dr. Connors. It's urgent," she said.

"Do you have an appointment?" asked the receptionist.

"No, but it's urgent," Pam said again. She gave the receptionist all her information.

"Hmm, let's see; well, you cancelled two appointments. Let me check to see if she is available." The receptionist picked up a phone, then turned back to Pam. "You're in luck. She just finished an appointment and won't have another one until 10:30 a.m. She'll call for you shortly."

Pam was both relieved and anxious.

"Hi, Pam, come on back." Dr. Connors led Pam to her office. "Have a seat. So it's been a couple of weeks since you were last here.

During your last visit, you talked about how the marriage was making you feel sad and lonely. Let's see … oh yes, you were assigned homework. You were supposed to write down all the reasons why you should let go and move on. Do you recall that?" asked the counselor.

"Yes, yes, I remember … but I can't leave him! I love him too much," Pam said in a soft voice.

"So tell me, what has happened since our last visit?" asked the doctor.

"Well, I didn't leave. I couldn't leave. It was just too hard. I invested too much," Pam said.

"You invested too much? How so?"

"Well, I spent a lot of money trying to look good for him … clothes, make-up, shoes, getting my nails and hair done. I have to compete with her. That other woman is ruining everything. She even told me he doesn't love me and that they share everything. But he told me he ended it with her. He told me it was over. Well, if it's over, then why didn't he come home? He's still with her … I know he is!" Pam whined.

"He said it was over? Did he tell you he was leaving her?" asked the counselor.

"Well, he told me it was over, but apparently it's not because he didn't come home last night. I know he was with her. I called him but his phone was turned off. How can he do this to me? It's all her fault. She's trying to ruin our marriage."

"Oh, I see. Pam, I'm going to give you a referral to see Dr. Brines. He's wonderful and will take great care of you. In the meantime, I want you to go home and get plenty of rest. Here, I'm going to give you a slip to give to your employer allowing you to take time off, if necessary."

"Oh, okay; well, thank you so much. I hope this doctor can save my marriage," said Pam.

After the counselor escorted Pam to the exit, she walked back to her office and picked up her phone.

"Yes, Dr. Connors here. I'm referring a patient to you. I'm afraid my services will no longer benefit her, at least for the time being. In addition to anxiety, I believe she may be suffering from some kind of personality or delusional disorder. She seems to believe she's married, but she's the other woman."

The Parking Lot

*T*his is ridiculous ... this huge lot and I can't
even find a decent place to park.

Angie circled the massive lot several more
times hoping to find a nearby parking space.
Annoyed from all the driving, she decided to
follow the next customer leaving the store,
hoping to find someone who would lead her to
a spot, preferably a close one. She noticed an
elderly woman and proceeded to follow her.

Oh yeah ... here we go. Angie rolled down her
window. "Excuse me, but are you leaving?"

"I sure am, Dear," said the woman.

"Thanks," Angie answered and rolled up
her window.

She continued to follow the old lady, who
suddenly stopped and looked around.

*Oh, don't tell me ... she forgot where she parked
... yep, she did,* Angie thought.

The elderly woman looked at Angie and pointed to a white compact vehicle on the next row. Angie tried to speed up to get over to the next aisle, but several pedestrians blocked her. A few parking spaces were available farther from the store, but Angie wanted the elderly woman's spot, as it was closer to the front.

Angie finally arrived at the next row and seeing the white vehicle slowly reversing, she drove faster. She pulled up near the car waiting to park just as a Mercedes swooped in and took the space.

"Are you serious? Oh heck no! No, you didn't just take my spot!" Angie shouted, blowing her horn.

Angie was so angry she didn't even notice another customer trying to get her attention that only two spaces away was an empty spot.

Still upset, Angie took the other space, jumped out of her car, and confronted the driver.

"Uh, you took my parking space. Are you that rude, blind, or just a jerk? Did you not see my signal lights on?" Angie asked.

The man's jaw dropped. "First of all, lady, I didn't see any signal lights. Then you ask *me* if I'm rude, when you're the one coming at me ... like a rude person."

"Oh, so you did *not* see my signal? That just

makes you a blind jerk," said Angie.

"Okay, seriously, all this over a space? You found one and you're still making a big deal over it. Thank goodness it wasn't a fender bender," the man said.

"It is a big deal! The point is the woman told me I could have her spot and then out of nowhere, you just took it. You think because you drive an expensive car that gives you the right to take someone else's parking space? You know, if driving etiquette school actually exists, you should definitely sign up, and hopefully, it will be a long course," Angie yelled.

As she turned and walked away, the man said, "Lady, you've got some serious issues."

~

After almost three hours of shopping, Angie left the mall and walked back to her car. She unlocked the door and slid in behind the steering wheel. As she put her key in the ignition and started the engine, a piece of paper tucked under the windshield wiper caught her attention. She got out of the car and snatched it up.

PARKING VIOLATION:
RESERVED FOR HANDICAP PARKING.

The Rebound Princess

I still miss him. I have got to find a way to get him back. Maybe I could give him a call to say hi. No, I need to say more than just hello. Maybe if he thinks I'm dating someone, he'll want me back. Yeah, that's it, Shay thinks as she stumbles out of bed.

She checks her phone, followed by a long sigh, seeing zero missed calls or text alerts.

After jumping in the shower, Shay searches for the best dating site, hoping to meet an incredibly handsome man who resembles her ex in any kind of form or fashion. She explores several sites, but no one comes close to Scott.

Time is ticking. Shay needs to find a date in order to carry out her plan. She creates her dating profile faster than a cheetah running on grassland. Several minutes later, a message from a man named Kent stops her in her tracks.

He is definitely not her ex's doppelganger, but he's fine enough to make Scott jealous. She sends an enticing message. They start a conversation.

Later that night, Shay stares in the mirror as she puts on another coat of mascara. Feeling quite satisfied with her appearance, she picks up her phone and purposely drops a text to her ex, hoping to spark his curiosity: LOOKING FORWARD TO OUR DATE.

He'll definitely call me after reading that text, she thinks. She rushes out the door to meet her new date at a trendy restaurant a few miles away.

"Kent? Nice to meet you. I'm Shay."

"Hi. Wow, you're much prettier in person!" Kent leans in to give her a hug. "Shall we?" He leads the way to a reserved table.

"This is a great spot. The food here is the best!" says Shay.

"Well, I'm still new to this city, so I did have a little help trying to find the best restaurants. I knew I'd meet someone but had no idea that I'd actually be on a date after just one message. So, how long have you been on 'Get to Know You'?" Kent asks.

"Not long at all … just signed up this morning."

"On your profile you mentioned that you're a foodie. So what do you recommend here?"

"Well, you've got to try the pan roasted chicken and the cauliflower with chili and garlic ... simply amazing!" says Shay.

"Whoa, I've never seen anyone so excited about food," chuckles Kent.

"Hey, I'm a foodie. What can I say?" Shay says and glances at her phone.

"Well, it sounds excellent; I'll have to try it."

Within seconds, a waiter arrives and takes their order.

Once the waiter is gone, Shay asks, "So, you're an accountant, right?" She checks her phone a third time.

"Yes, for five years now. This is one of the best states for accounting jobs. That's the reason I moved here. I've been staying with my cousin for about two weeks ... temporarily until I close on a condo I just purchased. Hopefully, that'll be real soon. Uh, I notice you keep checking your phone. Is everything okay?"

"What ... oh, I'm fine. Sorry about that," says Shay.

"No problem. Hey, our food is here. Let's eat."

After dinner, Kent walks Shay to her car. "I had a good time. Can I call you tomorrow?"

Shay's heart says no. Her heads says not sure. Her mouth says 'yes.'

"Great, I'll call you tomorrow then." Kent gives Shay another hug.

Back at home, Shay wonders why her ex has not called, especially after sending the earlier text. She takes off her makeup, jumps in the shower, and heads to bed ... with her phone close by.

The next morning, Shay awakens to the sound of a text alert. She jumps up faster than lightning, hoping it's her ex.

'GOOD MORNING, I ENJOYED OUR DATE. WOULD LOVE TO SEE YOU AGAIN ... HOW ABOUT LUNCH? THINK ABOUT IT. WILL CALL YOU LATER ... KENT'

Shay replies ... 'I HAD A GOOD TIME AS WELL. LUNCH SOUNDS GREAT. WHERE DO YOU WANT TO MEET?'

Kent responds: 'JASPER'S DELI? 12:30?'

Jasper's Deli ... that's perfect ... Scott's favorite. Maybe he'll be there and see us together.

Arriving right on time, Shay sees Kent at a table waiting to greet her. He gives her a big tight hug. "Great to see you ... you look beautiful," he says.

"Thank you. Is everything fine? You seem nervous," replies Shay.

"Everything is great. Let's eat," says Kent.

About half an hour later, Shay and Kent finish their lunch. "You're right ... those chipotle chicken wraps were excellent. Definitely must try the pastrami melt on our next date," he says.

"Next date?" asks Shay. She refrains from telling Kent the truth. In her mind, she wants nothing more than to get back together with Scott. And whatever is going on between her and Kent will only be temporary.

"Yes ... another date. I'll be a gentleman and pick you up. Look, I like you a lot. I know we just met, but I want to get to know more of you, and I'm looking for long term. Think about it. Excuse me, I need to find the restroom. Hopefully, your answer will be yes when I get back," he says.

Minutes later, Shay hears the sound of Kent's voice behind her speaking to a female. Their voices becomes louder the closer they get to Shay.

"I guess we had the same restaurant in mind. We were just about to leave, but let me introduce you to my date. Shay, this is my ex, Karen ... and her date, Scott."

Welcome, Ms. Parks!

"**H**ey Dad," Bernadette smiled into the phone.

"And how's my brilliant daughter? Are you ready for the big day?"

"I'm ready, but ..." she paused.

"You're worried about working with a bunch of men?" asked her father.

"Of course not. I grew up with three brothers, and a dad who owned one of the largest construction businesses in the country—which, by the way, I still can't believe you sold. It's just that being the new kid on the block at work and in a new city can be very challenging. Having to deal with the same old thing can be frustrating," said Bernadette.

A voice is heard yelling in the background. "Hey Fred, I thought you were going to hit?"

"Bernie Baby, it's my turn to tee off, but just

remember, relocating to a new city comes with challenges, but so do exciting opportunities. You're gonna do a fine job. And you've got what it takes to handle anything. Your mother would be so proud of you if she were alive. Let's have breakfast at The Dunch Cafe the next time you're in town? I could use another omelet. Now go get 'em, kid," replied her father.

Bernadette's call with her dad reminded her of why she accepted a new position with a large engineering firm; resilient and determined, just like her father.

Bernadette arrived in the building and took the elevator to the 9th floor. She stepped out of the elevator, addressed a couple of staff members, and walked into her office.

Minutes later, the firm's engineering manager, James, stepped into Bernadette's office. "Good morning, Ms. Parks. So, are you ready for the first official day?"

"Good morning. I sure am," replied Bernadette.

"Well, I see that you just walked in, so I'll let you get situated. I'm a phone call away if you need me," said James.

"Sounds good," Bernadette smiled.

She looked around her office space and realized how empty it appeared.

Could definitely use a little décor.

Bernadette reached into a storage box, took out a picture of herself and her English Bulldog, and placed it on the L-shaped desk. As she continued scrolling through her emails, she received a call on the company phone.

"This is Ms. Parks."

"It's James. I apologize but the staff meeting has been rescheduled for tomorrow at 9 a.m. I was just notified that a couple of employees will be out today, and I'll be conducting interviews for the senior engineer position in about an hour. The new hire will start tomorrow. So, as you can see, it made sense to reschedule the meeting."

"Yes, yes, I absolutely agree," Bernadette nodded.

Later that morning, Bernadette walked into the company's break room to get some coffee. A man she did not recognize greeted her.

"Good morning," said the man.

"Good morning," replied Bernadette.

"So, you worked here long?" the man asked.

"Actually, it's my first day. I'm ..." Bernadette was interrupted.

"No kidding. You know, they should hire more women; the more help with secretarial duties, the better. I'm interviewing for the Senior Engineer position. I'm very confident and can say I'm pretty sure I got the job. But don't worry, little lady. I won't make you fetch me coffee."

Bernadette calmly thought, *Since when did arrogance become the new confidence?*

The man continued boasting but stopped once James entered the break room. "Mr. Murphy, there you are. We'll conduct your interview in my office now."

"Well, good luck to you, Mr. ….?" she asked.

"Roger Murphy, but you can call me Rog." He gave Bernadette a wink.

It was almost 7 p.m. by the time Bernadette finished reviewing a few more documents and prepared to go home. She heard the sound of what appeared to be James ending a call on his cell phone. His voice was headed in her direction.

"I'm calling it a night. Today went well, and we've just hired Roger Murphy as our new Senior Engineer. He'll be joining us in the staff meeting," James said while putting his cell phone in his pocket.

"Oh, yes … Mr. Murphy … he's a very interesting character. Well, I'm really looking forward to meeting everyone tomorrow," said Bernadette.

"We're excited to have you, and welcome aboard, Ms. Parks," smiled James.

At 9 a.m. the following the morning staff

members chatted with each other as they waited for the meeting to begin. Roger winked at Bernadette as he glanced at her walking in the conference room.

James stood up. "Good morning, everyone. We have a few important announcements, but first, I'd like to make an introduction."

Roger fixed his tie proudly as if preparing to receive a standing ovation.

James continued. "I know some of you have met her, but for those who have not, I'll gladly make a formal introduction. I'm so thrilled to announce the top level engineer and president of Turp Engineering: Ms. Bernadette Parks."

Bernadette stood up and smiled, glanced at Roger, and waved, using wiggly fingers. "It's a pleasure meeting you all. We have a lot to cover."

Alternate Endings

Dear Jury

"Would you hold that door, please?" Staci hurried toward the elevator.

A man wearing a dark-colored grey suit held the door. "Of course, what floor?"

"Nine, please. Thank you," replied Staci.

After several seconds of silence, a weird sensation came over her, causing an undeniable urge to speak with the distinguished-looking fellow.

"You know, I find it rather eerie that we're the only two people in this elevator," said Staci.

"I'm harmless," said the man.

Staci giggled. "No … I meant that it's strange because we're in a courthouse elevator … on a Monday morning. It's just that I would have expected a crowd of people."

Just as Staci finished her statement, the sound of the elevator stopped on the 3rd floor.

An older man in a navy suit carrying a briefcase stepped in.

"Mr. Morris … ready for another great week?" asked the older man.

Staci thought, *So his name is Mr. Morris.*

"Always … strong team you've got there," replied Mr. Morris.

"Yep, and they're getting younger. See you later." The elevator stopped on the 5th floor and the older man stepped out.

As the elevator door shut and proceeded to move up, Staci tried to think of another way to start a conversation.

Maybe I can ask if he's an attorney. What a silly question. Of course he's an attorney … look at him; he's in a freshly pressed suit, carrying a briefcase … in a court building.

As Staci tried to think of another query, she actually found herself enjoying the comfortable silence and dropped the idea of asking anything.

Seconds later, Staci reached inside her purse to find some mints. As she dug through her bag, a few items fell on the floor.

"Oh great … why did I decide to bring this small purse?" mumbled Staci.

Before she could reach down to retrieve her things, the man was already kneeling to assist.

As Staci extended her hand for her belongings, their eyes locked just enough for her to notice the warmth of his eyes.

"Thank you," replied Staci.

"Of course," responded the gentleman.

Staci joked. "Your briefcase is a lot bigger than my purse. You want to trade?"

The man gave a faint smile. "Sorry, not today."

The elevator stopped and opened on the ninth floor.

"After you," said the gentleman.

"Thank you," replied Staci.

Staci stepped out of the elevator and walked briskly toward the restroom to touch up her hair and make-up.

Minutes later, Staci approached the area outside the courtroom. She waited among the other potential jurors to enter.

"I hope this will be quick," said one of the female candidates.

"If I'm selected this will be my first time serving. I'm kind of excited," replied Staci.

Before the two women could engage in a longer conversation, a bailiff walked out of the courtroom, made an announcement, and presented the court rules.

When the prospective jurors were escorted

inside the courtroom, Staci saw Mr. Morris, the same man from the elevator.

Staci and a few others were led up a few steps and seated in a jury box.

The judge explained the nature of the case, then proceeded to question each potential juror. After calling out several names, the judge finally made his way to Staci.

"Ms. Hill, it has come to my attention that there was contact between you and Mr. Morris. Is that correct?"

Hearing her name spoken by the judge, Staci's heart started beating fast.

"Uh, that's correct ... your Honor," she replied.

"It is very important that any incident occurring between an attorney and a juror has no effect on his or her ability to be fair and impartial. Do you understand, Ms. Hill?"

"Yes, Sir," replied Staci.

"How did you and Mr. Morris meet?"

"We met in the elevator ... this morning. I asked him to hold the door," replied Staci.

"Do you believe this incident will have any effect on your ability to be fair and impartial?"

"No, Judge. I ... I don't believe so."

"What was your immediate impression of Mr. Morris?" asked the judge.

"Well, I thought he was polite… and well-dressed."

"What was your conversation like with Mr. Morris?" asked the judge.

Please let this be the last question.

"It was not much of a conversation. Just small talk … like how empty it was in the elevator. Oh, and I asked if he wanted to trade his briefcase for my purse," replied Staci.

The other potential jurors chuckled.

"And why on earth would you ask such a question?" asked the judge.

"Well, it was just a joke because while I was trying to find some mints, a few items fell out of my small purse. Mr. Morris was a gentleman and helped me picked them up."

"I see. Just one more question, Ms. Hill," the judge announced.

Oh, thank goodness.

"Do you find Mr. Morris attractive?"

Staci felt perspiration leaking from her armpits. The skin on her face felt hot as if a blow torch was inches away.

"Excuse me, your Honor?" asked Staci.

"Would you go on a date with Mr. Morris?"

A few of the potential jurors snickered and giggled. Staci's face now felt like it was on fire.

Her heart beat even faster. She felt trapped and embarrassed. The uncomfortable position she found herself in along with wanting to be on a jury kept her from telling the judge the truth.

"Ms. Hill, you appear to be flustered," remarked the judge.

Staci words stumbled. "I apologize, Your Honor ... I ... I ... um."

Mr. Morris abruptly approached the judge. After several minutes of whispers between the judge and Mr. Morris, the conversation stopped. He walked back to the bench, and there was a stern—yet amused—look on the judge's face as stared at Staci.

"Ms. Hill, you're excused from this jury. The court attendant will escort you out with further instructions."

Staci was mortified. A variety of emotions overwhelmed her: anger, embarrassment, even relief, though the idea of not being able to serve on a jury was a disappointment.

Two Weeks Later

Staci walked into her flower shop, placed an 'open' sign on the front window, and proceeded to open the cash register while speaking with her cousin, Tiff, on her cell phone.

"I know you have to get back to work, Staci, but I just wanted to see how you're doing since that court situation," said Tiff.

"I'm good. Still can't believe that happened," replied Staci.

"You know, someone reminded me that something good tends to come out of what appears to be bad," said Tiff.

"And this someone wouldn't happen to be the Chubby Hubby guy you met in the grocery store, would it?" asked Staci.

"Kind of wild what missing ice cream will lead to," replied Tiff.

The two women chuckled.

"Well, it's going to be a full day, so I'll talk with you later," said Staci.

Although she was still feeling the lingering effects from the courtroom incident, speaking with her cousin always perked her up.

"A busy Saturday it's going to be. I better get moving on these orders," Staci told herself.

Thirty minutes before closing, Staci heard the ringing door but huge bouquets of flowers blocked her view from seeing the customer.

Like I said, a busy day …

"I'll be right with you," exclaimed Staci.

She walked toward the front of the store and

paused, her eyes wide open, then whispered, "Mr. Morris."

The well-groomed lawyer stood in front of the door sporting a clean and collegiate appearance.

Staci realized how girly she appeared and switched back to a professional grown woman tone. But that strange thrilling emotion she recalled feeling in the elevator snuck in. "What are you doing here?" she asked.

"I came to buy flowers," replied Mr. Morris.

"Oh. Well, feel free to look around. By the way, how did that case go?" Staci asked.

"It was a short trial … only three days. The first time I ever lost a case. By the way, you can call me Miles."

"I'm sorry you didn't win your case. It would have been my first time ever serving on a jury, but unfortunately that didn't happen," said Staci.

"I'm sorry you missed that opportunity, but there will always be more."

Staci sighed. "Thanks, but my chances of getting picked were probably slim to begin with. So what type of flowers do you need?"

"Well, I need to apologize to someone, so I would like the appropriate flowers," Miles said.

"Oh, I see … well, lilies and roses are perfect apology flowers. I'm a fan of the yellow ones, but

I'll need a little more details if you need help deciding." Staci walked toward several roses. "Is this for your wife, fiancé, or a significant other?" asked Staci.

"Actually, it's for a woman I met in an elevator a couple of weeks ago who didn't get the chance to serve as a juror. I'd like to get to know her ... and apologize."

Staci stood in disbelief and that odd sensation overcame her again. "I don't understand. What do you need to apologize to me for?"

He took a deep breath and released it. "You see, I was responsible for you not getting to serve as a juror."

Staci tilted her head quizzically.

"I asked the judge to dismiss you from the case," said Miles.

"But why?" asked Staci.

"Honestly, it would have been difficult for me to take my eyes off you in that courtroom, and that wouldn't have been fair to the jury."

Staci walked near the roses and picked out a bright yellow flower. "I think this should do it."

Sliding In Love

"9-1-1, for what city?"

"I'm in Madison Park."

"Do you require police, fire, or ambulance?"

"I need an ambulance."

"What's the address of the emergency?"

"I'm at Land's Park Trail."

Marianne was calm as she stared at her bloody leg.

"Can you tell me what happened?"

Marianne gave her name and said, "I was riding my mountain bike down a hill and tripped over some sticks and ended up sliding down a hill. A piece of the wood pierced my leg."

"When did this happen?"

"Just a few minutes before calling 9-1-1—around 10:15 a.m."

"I'm sending the paramedics to help you now."

Marianne released a faint moan. "Thank you."

She felt relieved that help was on the way. She called her parents, who lived four hours away, and gave them updates.

"Yes, I'm in a lot of pain, Pops, but I'll be okay. Let Mom know I'll be alright. Okay, gotta hang up now. The paramedics just arrived. Will call all you back once I get to the hospital. Love you," said Marianne.

As the ambulance pulled up, the pain from her leg became more intense. A lean male who appeared to be about 6'0 in height, stepped out the emergency vehicle and approached her.

"Hi. Are you Marianne Evans?"

"Yes."

"I'm Thomas. I'm a paramedic. We're gonna get you checked out, okay? I want you to relax and try not to move your leg for me."

Marianne couldn't help but notice the peaceful vibe that exuded from the paramedic along with the dimples perfectly placed on his chiseled face.

As the emergency driver rolled out a gurney, Thomas performed a complete assessment. "We're going to transfer you very carefully into the ambulance now."

Once inside the medical vehicle, Marianne

glanced at what appeared to be a 'hospital in a van.' She looked dumbfounded. "Wow. "So this is what the inside looks like."

"Your first time inside one of these, huh? Well, we want to make sure there won't be a second time," said Thomas.

Marianne's curiosity was sparked. "I bet you see a lot of accidents in your line of work." She pointed to her leg. "Anything like this …?"

"Oh, I've seen worse, but I love helping people. Hearing the report about a woman being injured from sliding down a hill was a reminder that I picked the right career," said Thomas while checking her vitals.

Marianne looked puzzled. "How is that?"

"When my younger brother and I were kids, we loved riding our bikes. My brother ended up sliding down a hill and falling off his bike, injuring himself. That was the day I knew I wanted to help people," explained Thomas.

"Is it just you and your brother? Do you have other siblings?"

"I have an older sister. How about you?"

"No, I'm an only child," replied Marianne.

Thomas continued checking her vitals. "Must have been pretty lonely."

"Yeah. It wasn't always easy finding friends."

"Ah. I know the feeling. I loved playing on

the slides at school when I was a kid, but I was teased by a classmate, so I tried to avoid the playground as much as possible. She picked on me all the time," Thomas explained.

"I think it was her way of showing you that she liked you. And you were lucky. My family was military, so we moved a lot. I hated it. It was hard to make friends," said Marianne.

"Sounds like we both shared something in common as kids—finding friends," said Thomas.

The conversation helped Marianne take her mind off the pain.

"So tell me, how long have you been bike riding?" asked Thomas.

"For a few weeks now … I like to find new locations once in a while. But love it here."

"I can definitely see why. The scenery is beautiful," Thomas said.

"You ride? You should visit," said Marianne.

"You know, I think I will. Well, looks like we're almost there," said Thomas.

Thomas quickly checked Marianne's vitals before arriving at the hospital.

"Thanks for the interesting conversation. You know, your childhood story gave me flashbacks of my own. I was so mean to this kid in elementary school, but it was actually a crush. Anyway, he would always pass gas everywhere; the monkey bars, merry-go-round, the slide. We used to call him—" Marianne was cut off before she could finish her statement.

"Art Fart?" asked Thomas.

Marianne eyes widened. "Yeah."

The Dream

"**O**kay, Ladies and Gentlemen, a reminder, your theses are due tomorrow afternoon. Please be on time for our presentation," stated Professor Mack.

The graduate students gathered their belongings and walked out of the auditorium. Professor Mack hurried behind hoping to get to an appointment on time.

As she approached her car, she heard the familiar voice of a colleague heading toward her.

"Professor Mack! Hi. Do you have a minute?"

"Yes, of course, Dr. Hughes, but only a minute. How can I help you?"

"Would you be available to speak at the academic conference next week?"

"I'd love to, but I'll have to check my schedule," she replied.

A Great Day for Ice Cream

"Great, I'll send you an email with more information. Thank you!" Professor Hughes smiled and waved goodbye.

Professor Mack unlocked her car door, slid in, and placed her laptop on the front passenger seat, and started the engine. As she pulled out of her parking spot, she saw one of her students, Sean, throwing a football to another student.

In the blink of an eye, screams were heard from nearby pedestrians, catching the professor's attention.

Suddenly, out of nowhere a vehicle came around a corner, leaving Sean crumpled on the pavement.

Professor Mack put her car in park, trembling from having witnessed the horrible scene.

As people gathered around, Professor Mack didn't move, too nervous to get out of her car. She was afraid of what she might see, but she wanted to make sure Sean was okay.

She finally stepped out and darted toward the crowd, but at only 5'3", it was difficult to get a good view. Then a voice shouted, "He's pretty banged up; call 911!"

~

BEEP BEEP, BEEP BEEP, BEEP BEEP. The sound of the alarm jolted Professor Mack awake.

144

She rubbed her hands over her face. "Wow. That was an awful dream."

An hour later, Professor Mack was dressed and ready to head out the door. The same tremble she had in her dream suddenly felt real. As she drove to the university, the accident kept flashing through her mind. The frequent quivers increased when she parked.

Another professor greeted her. "Good morning, Dr. Mack. Are you okay? You seem a bit jittery this morning."

"Yes, I'm fine—no wait, I'm not okay, actually. Let me ask you a question. What do you know about dreams?" she asked.

"Well, my area of expertise is accounting, so you may want to reach out to Professor Sanders in the Psychology Department. But generally speaking, I think dreams are all about the person who is having them," said the other professor.

"So, you're saying that other people in our dreams do not have any significance?" asked Professor Mack.

"I suppose. I mean, I once had a dream that a handsome movie star swept me off my feet. Guess what? No one has knocked on my door holding a broom," replied the professor.

They chuckled and walked into the building.

Professor Mack arrived in the auditorium,

took out lecture materials and prepared for a presentation. Her brief conversation with her colleague put her mind at ease, although she was still eager to see Sean, who was enrolled in her class that morning.

Students began entering the building and chatted with one another. As Professor Mack approached the podium, she glanced up and breathed a sigh of relief when she saw Sean sitting with the others.

The professor thought, *Yep, it was just a dream ... a silly dream.*

An Hour Later

"Okay, Ladies and Gentlemen, I hope you all enjoyed today's lecture. Now it's time to hand in those amazing papers that I'm absolutely looking forward to reading."

Professor Mack watched as the students paraded up to the podium one by one, with Sean among the last. He handed her his paper, smiled and said, "See you Thursday."

She piled all the papers into her briefcase and exited the lecture hall. She heard her name being called as she headed toward the parking lot.

"Dr. Mack! Hi. Do you have a minute?"

"Yes, of course, Dr. Hughes, but only a minute. I need to get to an appointment. How can I help you?" asked the professor.

"Would you be available to speak at the academic conference next week?"

Professor Mack paused, a weird feeling of deja vu recalling her dream. "I'd love to, but I need to check my schedule."

"Great; I'll send you an email with more information. Thank you." Professor Hughes waved goodbye.

Professor Mack was baffled, but continued on to the parking lot. She then caught a glimpse of Sean throwing a football and thought, *This can't be happening.* Mystified, she kept walking.

Suddenly, out of nowhere a vehicle came around the corner.

A frightened driver jumped out from behind the wheel. "I swear I didn't see her. She just walked right in front of me!"

About the Author

Kim Eve Bosley knows a thing or two about twist endings. In fact, four of the short stories in this book—"But, You Told Me," "Dear Jury," "The Dream," and "Thank You, Officer," were all based on her personal experience.

A former educator and government assistant, Kim writes fictional stories about unexpected events that everyday people encounter. She is also a podcaster, where she talks about real events with real-life plot twists and surprise endings.

Growing up in a military family, Kim wrote daily diaries on adventures that occurred in her neighborhood.

After graduating high school, Kim thought about working on a cruise ship or becoming a flight attendant for the travel experience, but instead, chose to attend college. She received a bachelor's degree in sociology, followed by a graduate and a postgraduate degree.

In 2009, Kim co-authored her first nonfiction book about personality types and human behavior titled, *Communicating Silence: What Our Wordless Messages Reveal,* with Dr. Mels Carbonell.

When she's not writing, Kim is probably reading or watching anything with romance or mystery, playing card games with her teenage son, or finding healthy recipes.

If you'd like to reach Kim, please email her at info@evestinytales.com.